Yorkshir

Saving pet

Nestled in a valley of the
village of Burndale, home to a very special veterinary surgery and its dedicated staff who care for and heal local pets and surrounding farm animals. Run by dashing Dr. Archer Forde, things at this quiet little clinic have always been straightforward—definitely not rumor mill worthy. Until the arrival of two new additions sets tongues wagging—and hearts racing!

Archer and vet nurse Halley were only supposed to have one night together, no strings attached. But now they have two surprises in store. Not only is Archer Halley's new boss, she's also carrying his baby!

After the loss of his wife, single dad James moves back to Yorkshire for his little daughter Tilly's sake. Joining his old friend Archer at Burndale Veterinary Surgery is just the fresh start he needs. A romantic entanglement is not! And yet the sparks that fly with vet Jenny are unexpected—and undeniable…

Escape to the country, rescue puppies and fall in love with the Yorkshire Village Vets!

Bound by Their Pregnancy Surprise by Louisa Heaton

Sparks Fly with the Single Dad by Kate Hardy

Both available now!

Dear Reader,

When Kate Hardy and myself were asked to come up with a cozy vet duet, we had great fun brainstorming our ideas. We chose to set our story in the Yorkshire Dales and I already knew that my heroine would be called Halley, after Halley's Comet. With this, it meant I knew something about her parentage and so I made her father an amateur astronomer, who used to take his daughter up onto a hill to show her the stars— a treasured memory for Halley.

So, when it came time for Halley to return to the village of Burndale, I knew this memory of happier times would draw her there and an idea formed in my mind of Halley meeting another great love in her life—our hero, Archer. Being on that hill would change *both* their lives in many ways. And I loved exploring the idea of how *one small decision* can greatly affect someone and I happily explored that in this book.

I hope you enjoy their story.

Louisa x

BOUND BY THEIR
PREGNANCY SURPRISE

———

LOUISA HEATON

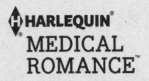

HARLEQUIN®
MEDICAL ROMANCE™

Recycling programs for this product may not exist in your area.

ISBN-13: 978-1-335-59524-9

Bound by Their Pregnancy Surprise

Copyright © 2024 by Louisa Heaton

For questions and comments about the quality of this book, please contact us at CustomerService@Harlequin.com.

Harlequin Enterprises ULC
22 Adelaide St. West, 41st Floor
Toronto, Ontario M5H 4E3, Canada
www.Harlequin.com

Printed in U.S.A.

Louisa Heaton lives on Hayling Island, Hampshire, with her husband, four children and a small zoo. She has worked in various roles in the health industry—most recently four years as a community first responder, answering emergency calls. When not writing, Louisa enjoys other creative pursuits, including reading, quilting and patchwork—usually instead of the things she *ought* to be doing!

Books by Louisa Heaton

Harlequin Medical Romance

Greenbeck Village GPs

The Brooding Doc and the Single Mom
Second Chance for the Village Nurse

Reunited at St. Barnabas's Hospital

Twins for the Neurosurgeon

Night Shift in Barcelona

Their Marriage Worth Fighting For

A GP Worth Staying For
Their Marriage Meant To Be
A Date with Her Best Friend
Miracle Twins for the Midwife
Snowed In with the Children's Doctor

Visit the Author Profile page
at Harlequin.com for more titles.

For our vet, Kevin. Thank you for
saving Mango's life x

Praise for
Louisa Heaton

"Another enjoyable medical romance from
Louisa Heaton with the drama coming courtesy of
life on a busy maternity ward. Lovely characters, a
great story, set in one of my favourite cities and an
all round easy engaging read."
—*Goodreads* on *Miracle Twins for the Midwife*

CHAPTER ONE

HE THOUGHT HE'D be alone.

He wanted to be alone. It was what he was used to, after all, and he was comfortable in his own company, so to come up here, to Rookery Point, and to find someone else was parked up here to watch the meteor shower? He kind of felt annoyed *and* intrigued. Annoyed that he'd probably have to get through an hour of inane, awkward conversation with a stranger, but also intrigued as to who it would be. It could be someone from the village. From Burndale. But he really didn't know of anyone else who was interested in the stars.

Archer didn't recognise the car. An old four-by-four with a large dent in the rear bumper. Switching off his own headlights, he killed the engine and looked up to the point and saw the silhouette of a woman, sitting on a blanket of some sort, whilst she fiddled with a small telescope. A stranger, then. But how did she know of this place? Not many people did, unless they were locals. He saw her turn to look at him, but he couldn't see her face because of how dark it was, though he thought he could tell she had long blonde hair.

It was the perfect night for staring at the sky. It was clear and cloudless. No breeze. The heat of the day still hanging on, so he only wore a tee shirt and jeans, though he did have his jacket in the car if it got cooler.

He got his own telescope out of the boot. His camera. Wondering if he ought to set up far away from this woman on her own, so as not to be intimidating, or whether he should just say hi, introduce himself and set up right beside her. He didn't want to be rude, so he decided he'd say hello, gauge how talkative she wanted him to be and then decide, so he began to hike up the hill towards the top. There was a small trail between the trees and he ducked to avoid branches and brambles and then he was passing Malcolm's memorial bench. Malcolm Campbell. Halley's father. This had been his spot. Where he'd stare at the stars, too.

Archer paused to stare at the words etched into the wood.

Dedicated to the memory of Malcolm Campbell Husband. Father. Dreamer.

He swallowed hard. He'd wanted so much

to be able to go and speak to Halley after it happened. To tell her he knew what it felt like to not have a dad. That she'd be okay. But he never could. She hadn't really known Archer even existed! They'd not moved in the same social circles at school. He'd been this weird, gawky kid with glasses and an air of neglect, whereas she had been…well…a goddess. Beautiful. Popular. Adored by all! He remembered sitting in the back of the one class they'd shared and staring at her beautiful hair, wondering what it might feel like to touch it. But he'd simply never had the nerve to *tell* her anything. Not even a *hello*, never mind a *Hey, you'll be okay, you know*. He'd not had a dad either.

He cleared his throat as he approached, just to let her know he was getting closer.

She stood up. Turned. 'Hey.'

And the moonlight lit her face.

Archer stopped in his tracks, heart pounding, not sure his voice box would work, but… 'Halley?'

She stared back at him, confused. 'You know me?'

'Er…yeah, I do… I mean…we went to…' He laughed, unable to believe that this was happening. Meeting the girl he'd loved from afar, for all those years, never believing he would ever have the chance to talk to her, ever, and yet…here she was. In this place. Of all places. On this night. Because she'd left the village. Gone to Scotland apparently, vowing never to return. 'Archer. Archer Forde. We shared a class once. Science. We dissected a frog. Well, you dissected it and I watched and barely spoke because you were you and I was just a…' He laughed nervously again and held out his hand in greeting. 'I work in the veterinary surgery in Burndale.'

She frowned as she took in all the information he'd just launched at her, but she reached out to shake his hand. 'I remember that frog, but I don't remember…' Now it was *her turn* to laugh nervously. 'You don't look anything like the kid I dissected it with.'

'Well, the years have been kind. Glasses got switched for contacts. Grew a bit. Fixed the teeth. Found a decent barber to tame the hair.'

'I can see that.' She smiled warmly, almost shyly, and it was as if his heart exploded in his chest and all the feelings he'd ever had for this girl came rushing back.

Archer had been the perfect angsty teen watching Halley from afar and dreaming what it might be like for her to notice him and be his girl. But which boy at that school hadn't?

Halley had been the most popular and most

beautiful girl there and her life had seemed as golden as her hair. She lived on a children's farm, so was surrounded by cute bunnies all day when she was at home. She had an older sister, Hillary, who was cool and clever and admired by all and they had a good relationship, so Halley knew all the older kids, too.

She knew how to wear the school uniform with her own touch of style and made it look good. She could sing like a lark, she got all the lead roles in the school plays, but she wasn't just beautiful, she was smart, too. Her hand was always up first to answer the questions. She did well on her tests and her exams. She loved to read and Archer could remember her sitting on the low wall at school some lunchtimes, with her face stuck in a book, her lips moving slightly as she read.

Halley's life had been amazing until her dad died when she was fifteen. In those weeks she was away from school, he'd wondered how she was. If it would be wrong of him to write her a letter, maybe? Only he'd never been brave enough and so he hadn't. And when she'd come back to school? She'd been different. Less sparkly. A little subdued. But he'd still loved her from afar.

'I didn't know you were back in Burndale,' he said.

'I'm not. Well, not permanently, anyway. My mum had hip surgery and needed someone to help look after her and run the farm whilst she's getting back on her feet. We don't need her slipping in the mud. My sister was doing it, but she's got kids and a full-time job, so…'

'So you came back to help? That's great. I mean, I'm sorry your mum hurt her hip, I knew she'd been in hospital, but… I'm glad you're back. I've not seen you since—' And he stopped talking because he felt she probably wouldn't want him to bring up the last time he'd seen her. Standing there, in the village church in her wedding dress, staring in shock at the woman who had brought an abrupt halt to her wedding.

Was she blushing? Halley looked down at the ground. 'Since I embarrassed myself in front of the whole village? I didn't know you were there.'

'I was at the back.'

'Well, believe you me, I'm not intending to stick around and have people gossiping about me again.' Her voice sounded odd. As if this wasn't what she wanted at all, but she was trying to be brave about it. 'I'm going to work the farm, help Mum and then, when she's better, I'm out of here. Back to Edinburgh.' Again, she tried to make Edinburgh sound as if it was her safe place, her home, but her voice was strained.

'Edinburgh? That's where you're living?'

'Living. Working.'

'What do you do?'

'I'm a trained veterinary nurse, actually, so, same industry as you.'

A veterinary nurse? He wished he had a vacancy at the practice so he could hire her, but they didn't. The only vacancy he'd filled lately was one of partner. Max had retired and now an old college friend, Jenny, was going to join him.

'That's great!'

She nodded and an awkward silence descended.

'So, I guess your sister is watching your mum right now?'

'Yes. They both knew how much I wanted to come and see this.'

These were the most words he had ever said to her, and he knew he had so many more trapped inside him that he could never say to her. Could never say to any woman, but especially not her. Sticking to the obvious seemed better. 'So, you're here to watch the meteor shower?'

She nodded. 'I am. You?'

'Yeah. Would you mind me setting up next to you?'

She smiled. 'Not at all. It'll be nice to have the company.'

Watching the meteors skim the surface of the Earth's atmosphere was the most beautiful thing she had ever seen in this world. There was just something magical about sitting there and staring up at the sky and feeling that sense of wonder. Of watching something leave a glittering silver trail of sparks in the darkness. A brief moment of beauty in the dark. It made Halley realise how all her concerns were just so petty. How little they actually mattered.

When she'd first left, she'd not wanted to return to Burndale ever. This village simply reminded her of all the terrible things that had happened in her life. All the heartbreak and the humiliation and the longer she could stay away from it, the better! But then Mum had had her fall, slipping in mud on the farm, and Hillary had called to say she couldn't cope on her own and it wasn't fair and that Halley had to come back and take on her share of the caring responsibilities. The farm was getting neglected and it needed work and Hillary couldn't do it.

I've got the twins to look after and Ste-

phen's on the oil rig for at least another three months! Please, Halley! Come home. Mum would love to see you, and you know how to look after those animals better than me, anyway. You're trained and qualified. You've got the knack. You always have.'

There had never been a knack. Hillary had just always preferred different things. The finer things that didn't include muck and manure and birthing baby animals in the middle of the night.

Halley had loved all of that, but, more than watching baby goats being born, she'd enjoyed the hours in the middle of the night that she'd shared with her dad, watching it happen. That was their special time. Just her and her dad, whilst Mum and Hillary slept. She'd get up and don her coat and wellies and they'd sit and talk in the barn, whilst waiting for a labouring mother to do her thing.

But if only I'd noticed the pain he carried. Why didn't I? Why do I never see the truth in people's hearts?'

Suddenly, three or four meteors skimmed across the sky. 'Wow! Beautiful.'

Halley turned and smiled at Archer. *He* certainly was. Nothing like the boy she remembered from the frog dissection, who'd been quiet and gangly, with a wild mass of frizzy, blond-brown curls. The boy who'd hardly ever been at school, if she remembered him correctly. Now why was that? She couldn't quite remember.

Now his light brown hair was tamed. Short. His eyes sparkling. Jawline square. A short, trimmed beard. He was cute! More than cute. The type of guy who she would let buy her a drink in a bar. A guy who was so easy to talk to. As though she knew him. Which, she guessed, she kind of did.

Why don't I remember much about him?

'You know I used to come up here with my dad?'

He nodded. 'Is that why you had the bench put up here?'

'Yeah. He used to love showing me the stars. Pointing out Orion, the constellations, telling me how they got their names.'

'I used to clamber out onto the flat roof of our house and stare at the stars.'

'Your parents didn't do it with you?'

'No. I never knew my dad and Mum was always too sick. Whenever I needed a break from her, or my little brother, I'd go out there, if the sky was clear, and look up. I didn't get a telescope until I was fourteen. I saved for it, bought it second- or third-hand with my own money after I took on a paper round.'

She nodded, trying to recall if she remembered him. But she couldn't see him at all. 'Did you whizz around the village on a bike?'

'I never had a bike.'

'Never? Whereabouts in the village did you live?'

'Opposite side to you. On Crab Apple Lane?'

She didn't say anything about how he knew where she lived. Most people knew she grew up on Campbell's Children's Farm. Crab Apple Lane was located on the other side of the village.

'I guess we moved in different circles?'

'We most certainly did.'

'We don't now,' she said with a smile. 'You work with animals. So do I. You like gazing up at the universe. So do I. You're here on Rookery Point. Alone. With me.'

'Yeah.' He looked at her so wistfully then, she felt something hit her squarely in the gut and she realised, with shock, that it was utter lust overtaking her. Whether that was because of the way he looked, or the romantic nature of having stared at the stars together, or because they were alone, up here, on blankets on Rookery Point…or because she'd not been with a guy for so long and felt a primeval urge to do something stupid and reckless, she didn't know. But she did know she was having the feelings with him looking at her the way that he was.

He liked her, too. She could tell. But this could be all kinds of dangerous unless she took control of it.

'Are you single, Archer?'

He stared back. 'I am.'

'So am I.'

He continued to meet her gaze, trying to read her intentions.

'You know, it strikes me that we could take advantage of this unique situation.'

Archer looked a little flustered. 'What did you have in mind?'

She smiled, unable to believe she was going to propose such a thing, but she believed in making her own luck. Grabbing at life when it was offered, because you never knew when you might get a chance ever again. 'Like I said, we're here alone. On blankets. It's a beautiful night. We're both single. Some might say this is romantic…'

'What would *you* say?' he asked, his voice low.

'I'd agree, but… I'm not looking for romance, just so you know. I'm not looking for a relationship. I don't do those—'

'Neither do I.'

'But…'

'But?' He was staring intently at her, his bright sparkly eyes now dark and dangerous.

'What do you think to the idea of a kiss? A kiss between two relative strangers who've met on a hill beneath the stars, in a one-time-only deal?'

'A kiss?' His voice had changed. Grown more husky. She liked it. She liked it a lot.

'A kiss. Nothing more.' She smiled at him, wondering what he might taste like, this boy she had once known, yet forgotten about. This boy she had dissected a frog with. This boy who had grown into a fine, handsome figure of a man, who she knew liked her a lot. Some-one she suddenly wanted to play with.

Why not do something crazy? She'd always stuck to the rules! Always behaved! And look how that had worked out for her. She'd done what was expected and had had it thrown in her face. Why not do the unexpected? Why not be crazy? Just this once? Kiss him as if she knew him, knowing she'd never have to see him ever again? There was no way she could stay in Burndale. She was here on reprieve. For a few months. Nothing more. What was the risk? It was fun. Just fun. And it had been a long time since she'd had any fun. It might make her time here in Burndale bearable. If she saw him. In the street. A fleeting glance.

The memory of what they'd done up here… A secret. Just between the two of them…

'Just one kiss…' he said, as if taking his time with the idea, as if he, too, was looking for the dangers of it. As if he, too, was wondering about how crazy it would be to do something so random and out of character? Not that she could know if this was out of character for him, but she hoped it would be, because if it was a rare thing, then he'd always remember it, wouldn't he? As *she'd* remember this night. Because she would.

I'll make sure to always remember Archer Forde from now on.

She leaned in towards him, smiling, almost laughing, watching the play of emotions cross his face, their lips inches apart. He smelt good.

He wanted it. He wanted her. But there was fear. Hesitation.

And she liked that. It made her want it even more. To touch him. Taste him. To be the one with the power. The one with the control.

One kiss and then, like a fairy-tale princess, she could disappear back to her farm and never see the handsome prince ever again.

She could do that. She knew she could. She'd had years to train herself to not get attached to guys. Years to not let her silly romantic heart run away with ideas of happy ever afters and all that nonsense, because she knew now. Knew they didn't exist. Knew they'd never existed! They were a fallacy. A trick. A trap she'd fallen into believing before and would never do so again.

But a little bit of lust? A little bit of daring and temptation? That she could deal with. Because she was making the rules and there was no way this could go wrong.

And as his lips came closer to hers, she fully believed that. Smiling, feeling as though she had won, as his mouth neared hers. And then he stopped. Millimetres away.

'You're sure about this?' he whispered.

She nodded. 'If you can keep it a secret. Can you?'

'I can. Can you?'

'Absolutely.' She moved closer. 'Why don't you kiss me, Archer? Kiss me like you've never kissed a woman before.'

And so he did and the second it began, she knew, almost at once, that it was never going to be just one kiss. Because kissing Archer made her feel as if the Earth had stopped revolving. That there was nothing else in the universe but them. On this solitary hill alone, beneath the ancient stars. That all that mattered was them.

And how he was making her feel.

Because she realised, far, far too late, that she never wanted this feeling to stop.

Two weeks had passed since the night on Rookery Point and Archer couldn't get it out of his mind. Two weeks since a kiss had become something *much more*. They'd left each other breathless and shocked and fastening their clothes, and though he'd wanted to call her to make sure she'd got back home all right, he'd refrained from doing so.

Nothing more can come from this, Archer. It was just this night, okay? What happened, happened. But that's all it will ever be.

'The one perfect night,' he'd said with a slow smile.

'One perfect night,' she'd agreed. 'Nothing more. No phone calls. No responsibility. No relationship. No falling in love.'

'No. Definitely none of that. I don't do that.'

He'd almost taken a step back towards her, but then she'd spoken again.

'Nor me.'

'Then we're okay?' He'd pulled his car keys from his pocket.

'We're okay.'

'Good.'

He'd helped her dress and, somehow, putting her clothes back on her had been just as erotic as taking them off! Sliding her jeans back up her legs, kissing her thighs as he'd done so. Pressing his lips to her belly, before the tee shirt had slid back down. Getting to his feet and stroking her cheek and planting one last kiss on her lips, before grabbing his telescope and heading back to his car.

He'd wanted to look back. Take one last glance. Absorb her in full, before he left, knowing this was his only moment with her. A crazy moment he'd cherish for ever. Only he didn't look back, because by then he was steeling himself. He'd got everything he'd ever dreamed of, but now it was over. They'd both agreed. Neither of them were looking for love. Neither of them were looking for something permanent. It could never happen. He'd been burned before. By her, even though she'd never known it and it had taken him a long time to get over the fact that she'd gone and left Burndale behind for good. There'd been one other woman. One other woman who he'd allowed to get close and he'd got hurt there, too. It just wasn't worth the pain.

At work, he got to his computer and called up the screen that showed the daily appointments to get a handle on what his day might be like. Letting his gaze scan the names and the pets and the...

Halley Campbell.

She was coming here? He clicked on the note beside her name. Saw that she was bringing in a trio of elderly guinea pigs for their annual check-up.

He licked his lips, trying to decide whether he should give her to Jenny, his new vet, instead? Let her handle her? But he didn't want to seem petulant, or childish, when he was a grown man and he ought to be able to handle one vet appointment. What would it be? Twenty minutes at the most? He could keep it professional. If she'd booked in with him and then she got here and found out she'd been handed over to Jenny, she might think he was ashamed of what they'd done, or was avoiding her after getting what he'd wanted, and he didn't want her to think that. Because it wasn't true. And besides, it would be an opportunity to make sure she was doing okay herself. Find out how everything was going on the farm. How her mother was doing.

See? Plenty of things for me to talk about.

Plus, it would give him a chance to look her in the eye. See her in the daylight. Become her friend as well as her vet. Technically, he had no doubt that she could do the annual health checks herself, what with her being a veterinary nurse, but the farm was a public farm.

It allowed children in to handle the animals and there were various rules and regulations that needed following and that meant getting a trained vet to assess the animals annually for temperament, diseases and health, to protect everyone involved. And they needed to be signed off by a third party. Not a family member.

Halley wouldn't be here until midday, so he could relax for a bit. He'd even get his morning break before she arrived, so that was good. He could check on how Jenny was settling in. He knew Jenny. Liked her. They'd met at college and become good friends after discovering they both were fans of James Herriot and watched all the shows and read all the books. It shouldn't have been a surprise to find another person who aspired to be the best vet in Yorkshire, but they'd laughed over a few drinks together in college and stayed in touch ever since. So when Max, the senior partner, had declared he was ready to retire and move to Portugal with his wife, Archer had advertised and Jenny had been one of the first to reply.

It had made sense to take on his friend. He'd felt as if he'd lost a surrogate father when Max said he was leaving to emigrate. So it was good to feel as if he was gaining back someone who he felt close to. Who he knew he could work with.

'We've got an emergency coming in,' said Barb, one of the receptionists, catching his attention.

'What is it?'

'Mrs Timball's cat, Felix. She thinks he's been run over by a car. She found him in the garden this morning and says he can't move his back legs. Feels cold.'

He nodded. 'When she gets here, send them straight through.'

'Will do.'

By the time Mrs Timball arrived just a few minutes later, he was ready with warming blankets and he quickly assessed the brown tabby. The cat was cold and a little wet from the morning dew of the grass, but it didn't feel as if he had any broken bones. All the joints and hind limbs worked fine upon manipulation. It was just that the cat couldn't move them himself, dragging them behind him like a puppet with its strings cut. Maybe this was a stroke?

'I need to do an X-ray, a scan, some bloods. Why don't you sit in the waiting room and I'll fetch you when I know more?' he suggested to Mrs Timball, who tearfully nodded, dabbing at her eyes with a white handkerchief as she returned to the waiting room.

Archer rushed the cat into the back room where the veterinary nurses were waiting and quickly and gently ran the cat through a battery of tests. X-ray. Ultrasound. Bloods. They gave Felix a shot of painkiller, just in case he was in any discomfort, but he didn't fight them at all. He seemed, if anything, resigned to his fate. He was eleven years old. A senior cat. But not so old that there was no point in seeing if there was anything they could do.

During the examination, poor Felix soiled himself and lost his pulses in his groin. With the scan results and imaging, Archer quickly had an answer to poor Felix's condition. He called Mrs Timball back into the examination room, where he had Felix lying on a warm, padded mat for comfort.

'I'm afraid it looks like Felix has a spinal embolism. In cats it's called fibrocartilaginous embolic myelopathy. On the imaging, we were able to spot a swelling and blockage in his spinal cord, causing Felix to lose control of his rear end. He's cold because he is losing blood flow to his rear end and there is evidence of progressive spinal damage.'

'So what do we do?'

'I'm afraid, in these cases, euthanasia is the kindest thing.'

'No!' Mrs Timball began to cry, hunkering down to place her face next to her cat's, stroking him and saying sorry and how much she loved him. She pressed her forehead to his and Felix softly closed his eyes and tried to purr. 'Are you sure there's nothing we can do?'

'I'm sorry. I can give you some time with him if you wish. He's on painkillers, so he should be comfortable if you want to call any family to say goodbye.'

'No. It's just me. And it wouldn't be fair to keep him hanging on. When will you do it?'

'We can do it straight away.'

She nodded. 'Okay.'

'Do you want to stay in the room? You don't have to, if you don't want.'

'This cat has been by my side for everything. When I lost my husband. When I got Covid. Everything. It's only right I stay by his side when he needs me, too.'

'All right.'

Archer gathered the medications he would need. 'This is pentobarbital. It will render Felix unconscious and then his heart will stop. It won't hurt him…it'll be like going to sleep.'

Mrs Timball nodded, tears dripping down

her face as she stroked Felix, not taking her eyes from him.

'Are you ready?'

'Yes.' Mrs Timball leant down and whispered, 'I love you, Felix.'

Once he was sure she had said everything she needed to say, he slowly injected the drug. It took less than a minute. Felix's head lay on the table and his eyes stopped focusing. Archer picked up his stethoscope and checked the heart, but it had stopped. 'It's done. He's passed.'

Mrs Timball's crying began anew and she began to tremble and shake and so he stepped around the table and draped an arm around her shoulder. 'Can I call anyone for you?'

She shook her head. 'No, love. There's nobody. I'm all alone.'

'What about a friend?'

'No. I'm all right. I'll be all right. Can I have him cremated? Get his ashes back?'

'Of course. I'll make the arrangements. Would you like to sit with him for a bit?'

She stared at her cat. 'No. Let him go. I ought to be getting back and, besides, you have a full clinic out there, you need to use the room.'

Mrs Timball wiped her nose and eyes with her tissue, sucked in a deep, steadying breath and gave him a quick smile. 'I'll go. You'll look after my boy, won't you? Make sure he's treated with respect?'

'Of course. As if he's my own.' Archer did have his own cat. Jinx. She was a rescue moggy. Pure black, with green eyes. Black cats were often the ones left behind in rescues or rehoming centres as some people were superstitious, even today. He knew she'd been mistreated at a previous home and he'd got her when she was seven years old. After she'd sat in the rescue centre for six years, being passed by every time. Well, he couldn't pass by, and she was the best cat. Affectionate, despite her past. A lap cat. With the loudest purr he'd ever heard.

He would treat Felix as he would treat Jinx. As he would treat any animal. With the respect it deserved. Each animal, each pet he saw in this practice was loved and beloved by its owners. They were family members and nothing less than that. They weren't just animals.

When Mrs Timball had gone, Archer took a moment to gather himself before his next patient. He'd always known that euthanising an animal was going to be the hardest part of his job and, though he'd grown used to steeling himself so he could deal with his patient's owner's grief, he still always needed a minute after, to gather himself and shake off the pain and upset that he had witnessed.

This was the hard part of love. The hardest part. Saying goodbye. Love was pain. He saw it every day. He experienced it every day. Loving someone who couldn't love you back? That hurt. Being left behind hurt. It was why he'd decided it was easier to not get involved. To stop giving his heart away for free, because every time he did, he suffered because of it and he didn't want to do that any more. His love had never seemed enough.

And yet still, despite hardening his heart, he felt it. Every loss. Losing an animal was hard. Losing a beloved pet was difficult and he saw the love the owners had for that animal. Witnessing their pain reminded him of his own and what was waiting for him when it was Jinx's time. He'd not wanted to get a pet because of it. Why put himself through that?

But he hated living alone and it was nice to have someone to come back home to at the end of a difficult day and animals were easier to love than people. They didn't hurt you deliberately. They loved you. Adored you. Wanted nothing more from you than what they gave themselves. They didn't fall out with you, or cheat on you, or deliberately go out of their way to lie to you or make you feel as if you were nothing. Or not good enough. Animals loved you for who you were and that was that. It was simple and Archer liked simple.

He scanned his list to see what was coming next. A dog with a mystery lump.

He hoped it was a simple fatty lump and nothing more.

He wasn't sure he could deal with any more heartbreak today.

Halley sat feeling nervous in the waiting room with her box of three guinea pigs—Milly, Molly and Moo—hoping that this visit would be simple. Easy. No making eye contact with anyone. Say hello. Get the three girls their clean bill of health. Say goodbye. Smile and go.

Why on earth did I sleep with the village vet? Of all the people I could have chosen, I choose the vet when I'm going to be working on the farm!

She knew she should have thought ahead about the practicalities of such a tryst but, to be fair, her brain hadn't been thinking of sensible things after lying on a blanket beneath the stars with Archer. She'd been thinking of other things. About how his hands looked adjusting the telescope. How square and strong they looked. How deftly he moved his fingers.

His biceps and how pronounced they were. The way his bottom looked in his jeans when he stood up to stretch. He was hot. Archer Forde was *delectable*. No two ways about it!

And she was a woman who hadn't been with a man for a long, long time and there was a need she'd felt to do something about that! And they were there. Together. Alone, under the stars. And it wasn't as if they were strangers, was it? She'd known him. Once, a long, long, time ago, and yes, maybe she hadn't noticed him, because back then he'd not been in her friendship group, but he was *gorgeous*, and she was a hot-blooded woman, and women had needs too, and…

You did it. It's fine. It was allowed.

It would be fine. They'd both set boundaries. A one-night-only deal and they'd stuck to that. She'd not heard a peep from him in the last two weeks since it had happened. No annoying phone calls bothering her asking for more. No awkward texts. No emails. No gossip whizzing around the village like wildfire. Clearly he'd got what he'd wanted from such an interlude, just as she had, and that was fine.

Even if it was the best sex I've ever had in my life.

Maybe it only felt like the best sex she'd ever had because they'd known it would only be the once? And so they'd both gone full out? Nobody normal had sex like that all the time, right?

She sighed and glanced upward at the clock in the waiting room. Each number was an animal. Twelve was a rooster, of course. One was a green snake, two was a chicken, three was a sloth, four a dog, five a starfish and so on and so on. Of course they'd have an animal-themed clock in here. Everything in here had an animal on it. The posters on the walls. The information leaflets. The stand in the corner selling dog and cat toys, treats and food.

Opposite her was Mr Knight. He'd been her headmaster at junior school. He looked old now. Silver-haired. Tired. But there was still that twinkle of mirth in his eyes as he looked down at his Jack Russell dog that lay at his feet, panting, quivering and shaking. Clearly the dog was no fan of being at the vet, either. Knight hadn't noticed her. Or recognised her, anyway, so that was something to be grateful for. Probably something to do with the sunglasses she had on, along with the floppy hat.

She'd hoped Hillary could have brought the guinea pigs. In fact, she'd promised to. But then one of the twins had been up all night with a fever and she'd rung first thing to say she couldn't make it over and that Halley would have to do it instead. She'd forgotten the time of the appointment and so Halley had rung to double-check and let them know that she was bringing in the guinea pigs instead. Maybe she wouldn't even get Archer? There was a new vet that had started, apparently, or so she'd heard. Maybe she'd get her?

But then the door opened and there he stood. Looking just as handsome as he had that night. Maybe even more so, because now she could see that his eyes were a rich hazel colour and, in his pale green scrubs, he looked even more attractive than she remembered.

Her heart pounded in her chest and she felt her mouth go dry in anticipation and so she looked away from him, not wanting to let him know just how he was affecting her, because she hadn't been expecting that.

I mean, maybe a little, because of how hot that night was, but this?

She tried to nonchalantly gaze out of the window to the street outside, but it was as if she could feel his gaze upon her and all she could think about was how his hot gaze had travelled over her semi-naked body that night and how he'd whispered against her neck how beautiful she was and she'd shivered and—

'Miss Campbell?'

She closed her eyes. He'd said her name. She

wasn't getting the lady vet. She was getting *him*. Archer. A guy she'd pinned to the ground as she'd straddled him and moved faster and faster until she was crying out as literal celestial rocks grazed the surface of the sky, creating fireworks.

She gave him a curt smile, nodded, and picked up the box with the guinea pigs and strode primly past him into the examination room, glad to be away from any prying eyes in the waiting room, placing the box onto the table that she could see was still damp from antiseptic spray.

Behind her the door closed. 'Good morning.'

The sound of his voice sent literal trembles down her spine. 'Morning.' She removed the sunglasses. Perched them on top of the hat.

'Milly, Molly and… Moo?' He smiled.

Grudgingly, she nodded. 'I didn't name them. They were nothing to do with me.' She laughed, not wanting him to think she was some kind of simpleton. Her mum had named them. Not that her mother was a simpleton, either, she just picked names that she thought children would like. If children liked the names, then they felt closer to the animals. Liked them more. Wanted to adopt them. It was a business decision. Sensible even. They made a decent sideline in animal adoptions.

'And how are they? Have you noticed any issues?' He stood in front of her now, looking at her, but she felt unable to meet his gaze. She kept staring down at the box the animals were in.

'Er…no. I think they're fine. They just need their annual check-up.'

'Okay.'

She tried to focus on his hands again as they opened the box. Inside, the guineas were huddled together in one corner.

'And can you tell me which is which?' He picked up the tortoiseshell one, with all the mad tufts of fur going in different directions.

'That's Moo.'

'Okay, Moo, let's take a look at you.'

As he bent down to examine the guinea pig, it gave her a moment to look at him unwatched. Unnoticed. He was tanned. As if he'd been away recently and caught the sun. He had a tiny brown mole on his clavicle, muscular forearms, and he handled the guinea pig gently and calmly, listening to its chest and lungs with his stethoscope, after examining its eyes, teeth and ears. 'Everything seems good here. How old is she now?'

'Erm…five years old. They're all five, I think.'

'Old enough for retirement?' He looked up at her, made eye contact and smiled and it was like being punched in the gut. She felt breathless. Unsteady. She placed a hand on the examining table and tried to breathe steadily.

'Yeah, Mum doesn't like these ones to get handled so much now. It's a young guinea pigs' game, apparently.'

He smiled and began his examination of the other two.

Halley was beginning to think she could relax. He wasn't going to say anything about that night, was he? And that was good. Because she didn't need him to. It was easier not saying anything. It would make the next time they met even easier. If there was a next time, but she lived on a farm, with lots of animals, so the likelihood was high.

But weirdly, she was also disappointed that he hadn't said anything. Now why was *that*? she asked herself. Did she want him to want her? Did she want to think that he'd been so affected by their meeting that he couldn't get her out of his mind and wanted more? As if she were some sort of drug? A mind-altering substance that he still craved? Because that would be a bonus for her ego, right?

That's all this is. Ego. I need to know that he was affected by that night as much as I was.

But that was all it was. Being *affected*.

It wasn't anything else. Because something that good *would* affect you. Wouldn't it?

'Well, they're all good. Milly could do with a nail trim, so shall I do that? Or are you able to do that back at the farm?'

'Oh. I can do that, that's no problem.'

'Good! Okay. Then we're done.'

'Okay.' She felt as if she ought to say something though. An acknowledgement? A reference to that night? Or just act as if it *hadn't* happened? 'Maybe I'll see you around?'

'Maybe.' He smiled and began tapping his fingers against the keyboard to input his findings into the animals' files on his computer.

'Okay. Bye, then.'

A quick glance. A quicker smile. 'Bye.'

And he continued to type.

The message couldn't be clearer. It really had just been one night.

Just as she'd requested.

Just as he'd insisted.

So why did she feel a little disappointed?

When it was exactly what they'd *both* wanted?

CHAPTER TWO

HE COULD BREATHE again after she left. How he'd managed to hold it together whilst she was here, he didn't know. He'd felt his hands trembling. Had she noticed? Thankfully the guinea pigs hadn't and animals were usually good at noticing nervous handlers. Maybe they sensed he wasn't nervous of them, but her?

She was even more beautiful in daylight. Her hair was golden. Honey-blonde and falling about her face in soft waves from beneath that crazy hat she'd been wearing, that he'd wanted to reach out and touch. Her eyes were beautiful. Her skin creamy, with a hint of pink in her cheeks. Her lips…*dear God, her lips*…were full and the most dangerous thing about them was that he knew how they felt upon his body.

But it was more than her looks. He'd always thought she was beautiful, but that beauty wasn't just on the outside. That night up on Rookery Point, they'd talked. Before and after.

She was funny. Kind. Thoughtful. They said never meet your idols and there had always been a part of him as a child that had told him that she probably wasn't as great as he imagined her to be, but she *was* and that blew his mind. There was nothing wrong with her.

Except for the fact that she was a woman who could hurt him again and, despite her being a goddess, he couldn't take the chance even with her. Besides, she didn't want a relationship either, so there it was, right there. She didn't want a relationship. She wasn't cut out for those. She'd told him, just as he'd told her the exact same thing, even though deep down he wanted something more. They were both done with all that, they'd said. They'd been there. Done that. Been scorched by flying too close to the sun. Burned.

And burns hurt.

Deeper burns seared away all those nerves and left you numb and unable to feel and that was how it was with him.

He'd tried to fly high and crashed and burned.

He would never try to do so again. Amy had seen to that.

But he didn't want to think about Amy. Right now, he just wanted to acknowledge the fact that he'd seen Halley again and that they'd got through it, without it being awkward, and she hadn't gone back on her word and asked him for anything he was incapable of giving her. Not his phone number. Not if he wanted to meet for coffee. Not any of that dating stuff.

They'd shared one hot night and it would be something he treasured for ever, but that was all it could ever be. He'd spent a night with the girl of his dreams, beneath the stars, and it couldn't have been more perfect and that had to be enough. It was enough.

It was...enough.

From now on, they would just be friends. Clients, if he had to go to the farm, or she had to come here with an animal. Nothing more.

Nothing more at all.

Halley hefted a bale of straw and dumped it down beside the others, cutting the twine and pulling it loose, so she could begin to cover the floor of the pen for the pygmy goats that she'd just cleared out.

This was hard work. Tough, back-breaking work and she wondered, once again, how her mother managed it. Her mother was much older, but she did this every day. Yes, there were farm helpers and all of that, but she knew her mum was very much a hands-on boss, who wasn't afraid of getting her hands dirty. She wasn't one of those bosses who sat in the office, punching numbers into a calculator and shouting orders at her underlings.

Halley had been here two weeks and already her back hurt and her muscles were sore and every night she fell into bed she was stiff, tired and exhausted. Sure that she'd have no energy the next day to get through anything, but somehow finding it.

Today was no exception.

However, it was fun and different from her usual work in a veterinary surgery. Back at Downlands Surgery, in Edinburgh, where she usually worked, she would either be sitting on Reception taking calls, or assisting in a surgery, or seeing patients of her own for six-monthly checks, or what have you. She'd always liked the practical nature of her job. That she wasn't sitting at a desk every day, that every patient was different and some of them were absolute mysteries until they could work out, like detectives, what was wrong and how an animal might be made better, if possible.

But being at the farm was good too. It was nice to be home, strangely. She wasn't in the village having everyone look at her with pity in their eyes, she was here. With the animals, and animals didn't judge you at all. Except to decide if they could trust you. And almost all of the animals here, with maybe the exception of Ivan the alpaca, seemed to trust her. They were used to human beings. They were used to being around them. Being petted. Being fed. Being looked after. A relationship with animals was more honest than any relationship she'd ever had with a human. It was simpler and she liked simpler. There was no subterfuge. No lies. No hiding. What you saw was what you got.

'There you go.' She opened up the metal gate that allowed the pygmy goats back in. They were Southern Sudan Goats and Mum had reared a fair number of them now. They had seventeen at last count and two of the females were pregnant, both of them with sets of twins, so that would take their total up to twenty-one, and Mum said when they reached twenty she'd swap some stock with another children's farm over in Cumbria, just to keep the breeding lines clean.

The goats tottered in, bleating, looking around before going over to the buckets that had their feed in on the far side.

Checking her watch, she realised it was breakfast time and she'd not eaten yet. She'd wanted to get these pens clean before opening and, now that it was done, she had half an hour before the farm opened up to the public at nine o clock.

Her stomach gurgled as if to remind her that she was, in fact, starving. She stepped through the metal gate, closing it behind her, then went over to the hand-washing station. One of many that were set up all over the farm, for kids to wash their hands. It meant bending quite low and she felt the strain in her back muscles, after hauling all of that straw.

But inside, she kicked off her boots and pulled off her navy overalls and headed into the kitchen to make Mum and herself breakfast. 'What do you fancy this morning, Mum?' Before Halley came home to help, Hillary had arranged for a bed to be set up downstairs, so their mum didn't have to manage the stairs. That wasn't needed now. Mum could make it up the stairs, if she took her time. She just needed to build up her strength.

'Eggs.'

'Okay. Scrambled? Poached? Fried?'

'Scrambled, please, love. On toast. One slice though, for me.'

'You'll have two. Keep your strength up. You've got that physio appointment this afternoon, remember?'

'All right, two, then.'

Halley smiled. Mum could sometimes be a

stubborn patient and Hillary said they'd had one or two fallings out since she'd come home from the hospital, but that was only because her mum didn't like giving up control of the farm and wanted to do everything herself.

'Everything okay out there?'

'Yes. Absolutely fine. Just as it was yesterday and the day before that.'

'And you know you've got the vet coming over late this evening to check on Bubbles?'

Halley paused mid-stride to turn and face her mum. 'What? What's wrong with Bubbles?' Bubbles was the miniature Shetland pony that they'd taken on as a rescue.

'Hillary thought she needed a check-up.'

'Wh-why?' She didn't want Archer to come here. She'd seen him only yesterday! He might think she was deliberately trying to see him again.

'Said she noticed she was lying down a lot yesterday and she's worried the laminitis issue might be back.'

'Well, I could check for that! We don't need the vet.'

'Well, I booked it already. I called them yesterday afternoon.'

Halley stared morosely at her mother. 'Which vet? The new one or the old one?'

Her mother shrugged. 'I don't know, love.

I didn't ask. Though it would be nice if it was Archer, I know him. Have you met the new one? Pretty thing, apparently. Was she there yesterday when you took in Milly, Molly and Moo?'

She shook her head. 'No, I only saw Archer.'

'Oh. Though thinking about it, it might be nice to meet the new one. Introduce ourselves. After all, we'll be working with them a lot.'

Halley slammed a cupboard shut after getting the bread out, and cracked the eggs into the pan, bursting the yolks and angrily giving them a stir. She added a splash of milk, a knob of butter and turned up the heat as the bread toasted. Her own appetite was diminishing by the second at the news of a vet visit. It seemed a complete waste of time! An expensive waste of time! She was a trained veterinary nurse. She'd be able to tell if Bubbles had laminitis. After breakfast, she'd open up and then go check that pony herself and when she discovered that she didn't have it and was absolutely fine, then she could cancel the visit.

Damn Hillary and her belief that what Halley did for a living wasn't a real job. Her older sister was a solicitor and felt as if she were the only one that had trained and studied hard for her living. To Hillary, Halley was nothing more than a glorified healthcare assistant. Something anyone could do. Well, she was wrong!

The toast popped out of the toaster and she placed it on two plates, spread butter on, then added the now scrambled eggs on top. She took the two plates over to where her mother sat, then she went to sit at the table to eat her own breakfast, but, even though she'd been starving earlier and looking forward to something to eat, the eggs tasted awful. Metallic. And the smell was beginning to turn her stomach.

Damn Hillary and her interfering!

This was her fault.

Archer pulled up at Campbell's Children's Farm, parking in the main car park beside the barn. He'd been here a couple of times, usually called over by Halley's mother. He liked Sylvie. She was a good woman, who ran a damned fine farm, educating children and their parents on farm life, animals and maintaining a healthy environment for all. He'd always enjoyed his previous visits, chatting with Sylvie. He wondered if she was up and about enough to speak with him today, or whether he'd get one of the daughters.

Whether it would be Halley.

Her visit to the surgery the other day had

felt a little awkward, but it had gone without event, which was good. That first meeting after having shared what they had was always going to be weird. But now he might see her again. Would it ever get easier? Would it ever be *comfortable* with her?

He killed the lights and turned off his engine and looked out to his right, where he could see a figure working in the barn. He instantly saw it was her filling up water troughs with a hose. Her golden hair gleaming in the lamplight. She glanced briefly in his direction then turned away again. He felt his heart rate accelerate and he turned away to take a breath, to tell himself to calm the hell down.

It's all going to be fine.

He walked to the rear of his vehicle, donned his wellies, grabbed his go-bag, squared his shoulders and then began to walk towards the barn, his gaze on her, taking in what he could before she turned. She wore fitted blue jeans, scuffed with mud, aged black boots, a tee shirt with a flannel shirt over the top. Her hair had been twisted up into a messy bun and strands of gold fell down beside her face, which, now he was closer, he could see had a smear of dirt across her cheek. 'Hey, good evening.'

She glanced at him. 'Hi. We must stop meeting like this.' She went over to a tap and turned it off, draping the hose over a hook on the wall.

He smiled, hoping she was just joking. 'These things happen.'

'I don't know why my mum called you. I was able to check the pony myself.'

'And what were your findings?'

She stared at him as if she were struggling to admit them. 'Laminitis. The pony's had it before, I believe.'

She had. He'd checked the file before leaving. 'Once before, yes. Want me to take a look, just to confirm?'

'Knock yourself out. If I'd had any spare anti-inflammatories from before I wouldn't have called you out at all.'

'Understandable.' He was beginning to get the feeling that she didn't want him here. Which hurt, but was fine. These visits here for him were difficult too. He'd made love to this woman on a hilltop. This woman he'd loved for years, ever since he was a little boy. Being with her was like fulfilling a lifelong dream and now she was talking to him as if he was an inconvenience? 'Where's Bubbles at right now?'

'I've got her in the stable. Follow me.'

Archer hated being made to feel as though he was an inconvenience. He'd had that his entire childhood. His mother had made him feel as though he and Axle were mistakes she'd made with their father. That she'd been left with the burden of raising them, after their dad abandoned them all, and she resented their existence, barely finding the energy to interact with them if the TV was on. He'd felt desperate for a smidgen of her love, which she'd given rarely and only when she was on her full meds and got straight.

But most of the time? He'd lived without it. Without his mother's love. Taking responsibility for his younger brother and making sure that *he* didn't feel as if no one loved him. His mother had made him feel as if her life would have been a whole lot easier without him around. Exactly how Halley was making him feel right now. As if she'd made a terrible mistake and regretted it. He was sensitive to feelings such as those. Maybe too sensitive? He tried to shrug it off. He was here to do a job.

Halley led him to one of the stables, where the pony, Bubbles, waited. She was lying down on the wood shavings as they entered.

'It seems to be mostly in her front hooves.'

'Okay. I'll take a look.'

He concentrated on the pony. He would show Halley that she might not want him there, she might regret that he was there, but he would prove that it was *important* for him to be there. He knelt to check the pony's hooves, gently examining them all, to see which were affected, which were worse, and Halley was right. The two front hooves were hot and tender.

'I've put her in here with a deeper bed of wood chips to help.'

'That's good.'

'And when I muck her out I put her in a bay with a rubber mat.'

'Sounds like you're doing everything you can.'

'I'm trying. But if you could just prescribe some more anti-inflammatories, that'd be great, and I'll get her started on them right away.'

She was trying to hurry this thing along. Get rid of him. He looked up at her and raised an eyebrow. 'Let me do a complete examination first. I'm here, might as well get the most out of me.'

She smiled, but it didn't reach her eyes. And it was brief. Too brief. There, then gone in an instant. Clearly he was making her uncomfortable. She seemed angry, almost. Should he be pleased at that? That their night together had had some sort of impact on her? Or should he be upset? Normally he'd like to think that if he'd been with a girl and she'd enjoyed herself, she'd be pleased to see him again, so why was Halley being like this? They'd had a great time. An amazing time!

'Does she need an X-ray?'

'Let's try the medications first and if that doesn't help, then maybe we should. Also it might be worth you calling the farrier to trim the hooves often.'

'He's coming tomorrow.'

'Well, then, you're doing everything you can. She's not overweight, so that's good. You don't have to worry about slimming her down. Let her rest. Maybe keep her away from the kids until she's better. And I've brought some anti-inflammatories with me, just in case, so I'll give you those so she can get started on them right away.'

'Thank you.' She sounded relieved now. Relieved the appointment was over?

He decided he needed to address the elephant in the room. He did that now. He'd been silenced so much as a child, as an adult, he liked to address problems and have his say. 'You know…we can be civil to one another.'

She looked at him. 'How do you mean?'

'I rather get the feeling you don't want me here. After what happened between us.'

She seemed uncomfortable at him mentioning it. 'Nothing happened.'

'But it did. We slept together. Unexpectedly, yes, but I'm not going to regret it. I, for one, thought it was rather beautiful and I will cherish the memory of that night, but you're making it difficult for me to enjoy it.'

'How do you mean?'

'Well, you can barely meet my eye, and you're making me feel like *you'll* feel a whole lot better if I just left.'

'I just… I don't do that sort of thing. Sleep with a guy I barely know. I try to get to know him a bit before I…' She seemed to colour. Blush.

He found it adorable. 'We got to know one another a little.'

'I know, it was just…impulsive and out of character for me and… I just don't want to make any more mistakes with my life, you know?'

'You're saying I was a mistake?' That hurt. His mum had once told him that he and Axle were both mistakes. Mistakes she regretted. It had taken him a long time to get over that admission from her, so he most certainly did not need to hear that from Halley, too. Not about something that he'd thought was so beautiful, because how could something so wonderful as their liaison be anything but?

She stared back at him. 'Yes.'

'Then I'm sorry you feel that way.' He marched away, unable to believe that she would say such a thing. He had feelings, he wasn't a rock. That night, however unexpected, however surprising, however brief, had meant something to him. And no matter what *she* said, he would cherish it and not let her cheapen it by calling their union a mistake.

It could never be a mistake.

Not with *her*.

Halley felt bad after he left. It left a sour feeling in her stomach. She'd not meant to say he was a mistake, but now he'd gone thinking that she thought of him with regret. It wouldn't do wonders for his masculinity, but what could she do? Tell him the truth? Tell him that, in moments of quiet, her mind kept returning to that night and dreaming of how he'd made her feel? And how she'd love to feel that way again? How in a perfect world she would return here to Burndale and maybe they might be able to have a chance, if she was brave enough?

Archer had treated her body and her soul

with reverence. That night had not been a passionate quickie under the stars, it had been more than that. Much more. It had been as if…as if she'd known him for years. He had touched her as if he loved her. As if he adored her. As if she were precious and he were going to savour every infinite moment with her. She'd felt special. He'd made her feel that way, that she was the centre of his universe, and she'd never been made to feel that way before with a man. Not even with Piotr. No wonder she still craved it!

What she hated was the fact that he had left an impression on her. Archer had left her wanting to feel more of that. Craving more of that. He'd intrigued her and left her thinking of him all the time and she didn't want that. It terrified her what that meant. Because the last time she'd felt that way about a guy—about Piotr—she'd been left with pie on her face. Jilted at an altar. The subject of ridicule and village gossip and pity. And she *refused* to feel that way again. Her whole love life had been exposed to the village of Burndale and they'd witnessed her fall. Her humiliation. And she would not embarrass herself again, in front of them, with the village veterinary surgeon!

'Was it laminitis?' her mother asked as Halley came in, pulling off her wellington boots.

'Yes.'

'Poor thing. Did he give you medicine?'

'Yes.' She shrugged off her jacket and hung it up on the hooks by the front door and dropped into a sofa, filled with cushions.

'You look tired, love.'

'I am. I'm exhausted.'

'What's for dinner?'

Dinner. Now she had to cook dinner? No wonder Hillary couldn't keep up with this. Running a farm and being a carer. 'I don't know. Something quick. Pasta?'

Her mother nodded and picked up her book. Some romantic saga she was reading. Not Halley's thing. It looked a thick book. Maybe five hundred pages? 'Whenever you're ready.'

'I might just close my eyes for five minutes.'

Her mother glanced at her. 'Not too long though, love.'

'No. Not too long.' She allowed her eyes to close and fell into a deep sleep, almost instantly. She dreamed of Archer, of course. Him and her, back on Rookery Point, beneath the stars and she was holding his hand, staring up at the sky. Neither of them saying anything. Just being together and it being enough. And she turned to look at him as he said, 'Halley, I need you to wake up now. Halley!'

And she jumped, because it wasn't his voice, but her mother's, and when she blinked her eyes open, her mother was staring at her, frowning.

'I'm sorry…what?'

'I'm starving, love. I'd do it, but you'd tell me off, so… Can you make us something to eat?'

'Sure. Sure.' She scrambled to her feet, trying to feel awake as she stood.

'You talk in your sleep, you know.'

Halley turned around in the kitchen doorway. 'Do I? Did I say anything vaguely sensible?'

'You were muttering about the vet, I think. You kept saying Archer.'

'Oh.'

'You must have been worrying about Bubbles way more than you thought!'

Halley smiled. 'Yes. That must be it.'

Her mother smiled back. 'Bless your heart.'

She thought he'd been a mistake. Well, that hurt, because he would never think of what they had done as a mistake. Even though he'd known, at the time, that it was something that would never be repeated, because they'd both stated that quite clearly. Neither of them wanted anything to come of their…interaction. But he would never call what they did a mistake.

To him, it had been a beautiful thing. Something he would cherish for ever. He would never think of Halley Campbell as a mistake, even if she regretted their association.

His brother, Axle, deliberately stepped in front of him to get his attention. 'Hey, are you even listening to me?'

Archer blinked and nodded, smiling. 'Of course!'

'Then what did I just say?'

'Er…you were talking about Joanne.'

'And?'

Archer grimaced. 'Sorry. You're right. I got distracted. What did Joanne have to say when you last spoke to her?'

Axle frowned. 'That she'd been offered a promotion in her job and it would mean longer hours and she couldn't see herself coming back to Burndale or even Yorkshire any time soon.'

'So when do you get to see the kids?' Axle had had two kids with Joanne, but their relationship had been problematic from the get-go, with issues over jealousy and lying, and they'd had an on-again, off-again relationship for a couple of years, before Joanne had upped sticks and moved to Cardiff, taking Axle's two sons with her. He'd barely seen them since.

'She said not any time soon.'

'But you can visit them?'

'You know what she's like, though. She agrees to let me see them, then I travel all that way for my appointed time and she goes out, or she refuses! The last time she slammed the door in my face.'

'You did turn up slightly drunk.'

'I needed a drink before seeing her. You know how she pushes all my buttons. I just wanted to spend some time with my kids, you know, is that so bad?'

'Of course not. You want to be a good dad. But, Ax, turning up drunk isn't going to get you that. You need to lay off having a pint with the lads before you go there. If she gives you a time to see the boys, then get there for that time, and if she mucks you around, stay calm and ask for another time to see them. Be calm and assertive, not aggressive.'

'I miss my kids, Archie. I don't want them growing up thinking they haven't got a dad, like we did. Or that they have a parent that doesn't care.'

'I know.' He laid a reassuring hand on his brother's shoulder. 'Has she said you can visit?'

'This weekend I'm going down to Cardiff.'

'Okay. Well, maybe this time it'll work out.'

'You said that last time. And the time before that. Do you think I'm going to have to take her to court just to see my kids?'

'I hope not. I hope you can work it out between yourselves.'

'Yeah. Me too.'

'You been speaking to the boys on the phone, though?'

'Not since last time. She won't put them on the phone and they're too young to have mobiles of their own, so I always have to go through her. Do you know how hard it is, Arch, to want to be with someone so badly and they just won't let you?'

Archer nodded.

'It drives me crazy! I should never have got involved with Joanne. She was a big mistake! I should have picked someone like me. Who wanted the same things as me.'

'You did what you thought was right at the time.'

'But it was never enough.'

Archer didn't know what to say. His brother was hurting, and he couldn't imagine being in a similar situation if he were to ever make the mistake of having kids. He'd told himself long ago he'd never have them, and it was hearing stuff like this that told him he'd made the right decision.

CHAPTER THREE

HALLEY WOKE FEELING EXHAUSTED, despite having an early night and sleeping for ten hours straight.

Maybe I've had too much sleep?

She'd read that once. That too much sleep could be as bad, if not worse, than too little.

Maybe it was all down to the physical work she was doing, not just on the farm, but also in looking after her mum.

She grabbed her robe and ambled down the stairs, frowning when she heard noises and music coming from the kitchen. 'Hello?'

She turned the corner at the bottom of the stairs and saw her mum, already on the couch reading a magazine, and in the kitchen, stirring a pan, was Hillary, her sister.

'Afternoon, sleepyhead,' said Hills, with a raised eyebrow.

Halley looked at her wristwatch. It was only eight-thirty. 'It's still morning.'

'And Mum needed her pain meds at eight. She had to call me to come over to give them to her, because she couldn't reach them from the high cupboard in the kitchen.'

Halley frowned and looked at her mum. 'You could have called me.'

'I did. You didn't answer. I got worried and called your sister.'

'Luckily, I'm not in court until this afternoon and I'd already dropped the twins off at breakfast club, so I could come over. I checked you were still breathing and then gave Mum her meds. I'm just doing her porridge, now.'

'Oh, well, thanks. I'm sorry I didn't hear you, Mum. I must have been well tired.'

Hillary tilted her head to look at her. 'You do look a little peaky.'

'I always look like this first thing.'

'Well, thank God you don't have a boyfriend, then—he'd run a...' She stopped. Grimaced. 'Sorry.'

'No. It's fine.' Halley activated the camera on her mobile phone and glanced at her appearance. Hills was right. She did look a little pale. 'Ugh.'

'You feeling okay?'

'Tired.'

'It's hard work, isn't it? Do you see now, why I asked you to come back and help me?

I've been doing this, the farm, Mum, looking after the twins and trying to be a solicitor! It's your turn, now.'

'I know, I know. Thank you for all you've done. You're Superwoman, Hills.'

Her sister smiled and bit into a piece of toast. 'I've put on enough porridge for you, too, if you want some?'

'Sure.' Halley settled down onto a seat in the kitchen as Hillary poured some porridge into bowls and set one down in front of her. Halley sprinkled some sugar on the top and then ate a mouthful, grimacing at the heat and the taste.

'Something wrong with it?'

'What have you put in it?'

'Nothing. Oats. Mum likes it plain.'

'It tastes…awful!'

'Well, thank you. You're very welcome,' Hills said sourly.

'Tastes fine to me, love,' said their mum, from the couch.

'Perhaps there's something wrong with your tastebuds then, because this tastes like…' She trailed off as she had a sudden rush of nausea in her stomach. It came over her like a wave and was then gone again, almost as quickly as it came. Halley pushed the bowl away. 'Ugh… I think I'll just have some toast, or something.'

'Ingrate.' Hillary took their mother a glass of orange juice. 'Right, now your actual slave has crawled out of her pit, I'll be on my way.' She turned to Halley. 'Don't forget to open up!' And then she was gone. The whirlwind that she was, out of the door and gone.

Halley stared at the toaster, waiting for her second choice of breakfast.

Why do I feel like crawling back into bed?

Lunchtime and Archer had popped into the local shop to pick up a sandwich or something. It had been a busy morning. A full clinic of yearly boosters, general check-ups and he'd even managed to spay two cats. He enjoyed doing surgeries. He liked the calm and the peace that came over him when he had to wield a scalpel. The operating room was like a different world from the real one. Where time slowed down and all that mattered in the world was the animal on the table and his own skill. It gave him a nice healthy appetite when surgeries and clinic went well. And after his visit from Axle, he'd needed a calming day. A good day. Because he'd been feeling out of sorts since meeting Halley on Rookery Point and hated that they'd had a little disagreement last night. But he'd needed to say something. He'd picked up a basket and was browsing the refrigerators and the sandwich selection, trying to decide between a BLT or a chicken Caesar, when the bell over the door rang, admitting a new customer.

His first glance told him it was none other than Halley Campbell, the girl who thought of him and their tryst as a mistake. The second glance took in the fact that she looked tired and a little pale. Two small spots of pink on her cheeks.

She didn't see him as she went straight over to the shelves where the medicines were. Painkillers, sore-throat lozenges, that kind of thing.

Archer selected the BLT and grabbed himself a drink, trying to steady the rapid beating of his heart. When he'd asked her to be more civil when talking to him, he'd truly asked it as a simple request. He'd not said it in a mean tone, or an accusatory one. But he hated that he'd had to say it at all. He wanted relations between them to be good. Especially after what they'd shared. Two people who could be that good together sexually ought to be decent.

'Do you have any antacids?' he heard her ask Ruth, the shopkeeper.

'Bottom shelf, love.'

'Oh, yeah. Thanks.'

He came up behind her as she went to pay

for them, standing there with his basket, waiting for her to be served.

'Five fifty.'

Halley reached into her coat pocket for her purse, but then stopped, pausing, closing her eyes to shake her head and groan.

Archer frowned, instantly concerned. 'Are you okay?'

'I'm fine. I'm just…' She reached out to put a hand on the counter as if to steady herself.

Archer put his basket down and stepped forward, reaching out to help steady her. 'Do you need to sit down? Ruth, can you get her a chair?'

She shrugged him off. 'No! No, I'm fine. I just felt a little weird, is all.'

'Maybe you need to see a doctor?'

She turned to glare at him, her cheeks flushing with anger. 'I don't need to see a doctor! I just didn't have breakfast this morning, that's all.'

He turned and reached for a chocolate bar off the shelf, ripped open the wrapper and passed it to her. 'Then eat this. Now. Ruth, you can add it to my bill in a minute.'

'I don't want chocolate.'

'Tough. If you've not eaten breakfast and you're light-headed enough to almost pass out in the village shop, then your blood sugar is low and chocolate is the quickest thing to raise those levels.'

She held the chocolate bar and stared hard at him. 'Actually, you'd be better getting me to rub honey or jam on my gums. That'd be fastest.'

'Just eat the bar!' he said, exasperated. Why was she fighting him on this? Was it her way? To be antagonistic on everything? Or was it only him that had this effect on her? He calmed his voice. 'I'm just trying to help you.'

'I don't need your help.'

'No. You need sugar. Now eat the chocolate.'

She stared at him as if contemplating another challenge, but decided against it and sullenly took a bite. Wrinkling her nose at it.

'Something wrong?'

'I'm not a big fan of this one.'

He smiled. 'I'm so sorry. Which is your favourite? I'll remember it for the next time.'

'There won't be a next time. I don't like to almost pass out in village shops.' She glanced over at Ruth. 'Don't go telling people about this. I'm enough of a talking point already.'

Ruth made a zipping motion over her mouth and smiled.

After a couple of mouthfuls, the chocolate bar was gone.

'Better?'

Halley nodded.

'Okay. Let's pay for the antacids and I'll walk you to your car. Are you going to be okay to drive?'

'I'm fine.'

'Maybe I should follow you back to the farm, just in case?'

'Don't you have work?'

'Yes, but I'd rather make sure you got home safely.'

'Look, I don't need you babysitting me and I don't need to be responsible for your clinic running late. How about you go back to your job and I'll text you when I'm home, so you know I got back safe?'

'You don't have my number.'

She pulled out her mobile phone, opened up the contacts list and then passed it over to him. 'Put it in.'

He typed his number into her phone and passed it back. 'No cheating.'

'I don't cheat.'

'I'm glad to hear it.' He stared back at her with a smile, glad that their relationship had changed from peeved and mistaken to tolerant and challenging. It was a step forward!

Archer paid for his sandwich, drink and the chocolate bar and followed Halley out to her car parked on the road. He watched her get in, smiling all the time.

'What is wrong with you?' she wound down her window to ask him.

'What do you mean?'

'I mean no one is this happy all the time.'

'Maybe you're giving me things to be happy about.'

Halley frowned. 'Well, stop it. I don't like it.'

He had to stop himself from laughing. 'I'll try to be more glum.'

'Thank you.'

'Until I get your text and then I'll be happy again.'

'Just go to work, Archer.'

Now he did laugh 'Yes, ma'am.' He gave her a salute and began to walk back to work.

Halley watched him go, silently cursing. What was it about him that was winding her up? That he challenged her? That he'd seen her semi-naked and vulnerable, as well as ill and vulnerable? He was always around! Or maybe that was just the problem with living in a village—you kept running into the same people. That was one of the only reasons Edinburgh was better. It was big enough to be anonymous in.

Here, in Burndale, you couldn't get anonymity if you tried. Everyone knew everything about you and, despite Ruth's assurances that she wouldn't say a word about Halley's little spell in the shop, she knew that by teatime plenty of people would have heard about it. It was the village shop and Ruth was a talker. Always had been. Always would be.

The idea that she'd be the number one topic once again did not sit well with her and so she ripped open the antacids that she'd bought and took a couple. That chocolate bar had taken away some of the nausea she'd been feeling, but it was back again. She felt hungry, too, at the same time. It was weird. The morning had been frightening too. She'd never passed out in her life! And what had that moment been? In the shop? She'd been about to faint or something…

It was down to not having eaten—it had to be that. She was doing a huge amount of physical hours now. Running the farm. Caring for her mum. Dealing with all the issues that came along with that, day after day, and not eating? Well, that was a recipe for disaster, right? And this nausea that she'd had for a couple of days? It wasn't terrible. It wasn't as if she couldn't deal with it, but it was always there. Low-level. In the background.

Maybe it's stress? I'm not used to it.

Whatever was causing it, she didn't like it. She didn't like feeling out of control. Even over her own body. Halley controlled every aspect of her life for a reason. So that she didn't get hurt again. So that she never had to go through something so publicly again. And could she do that if she was going to pass out all over the place?

Maybe I ought to get checked out.

It seemed the sensible, logical thing to do. Prevention was better than cure, or so they said. So, instead of driving home, Halley made the short drive to the Burndale Doctor's Surgery and made an appointment. She was lucky. There was an appointment for first thing the next morning. She'd go after opening up.

She'd probably feel better by then anyways.

He dealt with an ear infection in a spaniel dog before Halley's text popped into his phone confirming she was home safe. There was even a picture of her standing by the farm sign, smiling sarcastically at him.

He couldn't help but smile back and saved her details in his contact list. Another guy might consider this progress—getting a girl's number—but he didn't need it. It wasn't as if they were in a relationship or anything.

She was just going to be a friend. A reluctant friend, maybe, but a friend, nonetheless.

He texted back.

Now go put your feet up.

I've got too much to do.

When you're finished. Put your feet up. Or do I have to come round there to make sure that you do?

He added a couple of smiley faces and waited for her reply. Nothing came for a while and he was about to put his phone away and call in his next patient, when his phone beeped a reply.

Fine. I'll rest.

And she put a smiley face, too.

Archer put his phone away, feeling much better. Their relationship was in a better place than before, yet again, and all it took was a little mild chiding and a show of concern. Maybe she did let people in, after all. And maybe he did care, but so what? He was just being a friend.

He called in his next patient. 'Mango?'

Sarah Chalmers stood up and carried in her Yorkshire terrier, giving him a nice smile as she passed him by. 'Hello, Archer.'

'Hi. What seems to be the problem?' He closed the door to the consulting room behind them and came around the examining table that Mango was now standing on.

'Well, I've noticed she has this weird cough and seems to gag a lot. I'm afraid she does chew a lot of sticks and I'm worried she's got something stuck in her throat.'

'Okay, and how long has this been going on for?'

Sarah shrugged. 'A few weeks. I would have brought her earlier, but I've not been well myself.'

'I'm sorry to hear that. Are you better now?'

'Much. I had a chest infection and had to go on antibiotics.' She paused. 'I've not given it to my dog, have I?' she asked with real concern.

'Not likely. Let me examine her and we'll go from there. I'll just do her general observations first and then look in her mouth.'

He checked the dog over and found nothing of concern. It didn't have a temperature... its stomach was soft. Heart was good. Eyes clear and bright. But he could hear a rasping noise and when he looked in the dog's mouth, he couldn't see a blockage trapped there anywhere. 'Do you have anything in your home like scented candles? Or do you smoke yourself?'

'I don't smoke and do occasionally have a scented candle when I'm in the bath, but not often.'

'And I see you have a lead on a neck collar. Does she pull on walks?'

'She does, actually. Quite a lot. She hates big vehicles driving past and gets scared and she's always pulling to get back home.'

'Okay. Well, little dogs like these can sometimes have issues with their trachea, that can be exacerbated by neck collars. It's best to use a body harness, rather than something that can pull on their throat, especially if they're a puller.'

'Really? I never knew that. Is that what you think this is?'

'We'll need to do some bloods and maybe an X-ray just to confirm there's nothing in her throat that shouldn't be there. But I can give her some anti-inflammatories for now, just in case it's anything else.'

'And when would you do the bloods and X-ray?'

'Bloods we can do tomorrow, first thing. X-ray would be later on that morning. Could you bring her in first thing tomorrow and then we'll give you a call when it's all done?'

'Sure. Thank you.'

'No problem. In the meantime, why not try adding a little bit of organic honey to her food? It should help calm any coughing she's doing.'

'Okay, thank you, Archer.'

'No problem. We'll see you both tomorrow.'

She thanked him as she left and he closed the door to type up his notes to add to Mango's file.

Halley hated doctors' surgeries. More specifically, she hated doctors' surgery waiting rooms. Especially here, in Burndale.

The room was full of waiting patients, all of whom knew each other. All of whom knew *her*. So when she walked in, she felt all eyes turn to her, a couple widening briefly. Then there was whispering and she knew, yet again, that at least by lunchtime half the village would know that she had been at the doctor's that morning.

She sat in a corner seat and picked up a magazine to hide behind. It wasn't even a good magazine! It was one she associated with being aimed at older women. Filled with recipes, health advice and short stories. She tried to concentrate hard on some story about a woman who couldn't sing, but who got asked to join a church choir and found love on the way, but it was difficult when Halley heard her name whispered over to her right.

Her cheeks flushed and she raised the magazine higher. What a highlight it must be for these women! Halley Campbell, jilted at the altar, back home in Burndale! She bet they knew why she was back. Her mum's fall at the farm and her subsequent broken hip was old news. But Halley herself?

'Halley, love…how's your mother doing?'

She lowered the magazine to peer at an old woman she wasn't sure she recognised. But she was sitting next to Mrs Grigson, who was one of the nosiest people in Yorkshire! 'She's doing fine, thanks.'

'You and Hillary helping out at the farm?'

'We're trying.' She was trying to be polite, too.

'You were in Edinburgh, weren't you?'

'That's right.'

'Settled in nicely up there, have you?'

'Yes, wonderfully so.' She wasn't going to tell Mrs Grigson the truth.

'Oh, I am glad. After all that business with that man…'

Piotr. She meant Piotr.

'You're happy now?'

'Very happy.'

'Must be difficult for a young woman living alone in such a big city…?'

She was prying. Trying to find out if there was anyone new in her life. 'Not really.'

'I could never do it…oh, no. But then I don't have to. I've got my Duncan by my side and he looks after me wonderfully.'

Duncan Grigson was her husband of many years. 'I'm glad to hear it.'

Mrs Grigson leaned in with a smile. 'Have you managed to find yourself a nice young man? Pretty thing like you?'

Halley had to hold back from saying something startling and astonishing like, *Well, I screwed the vet on top of that hill a couple of weeks ago…he was nice*. But she chose not to. It might be nice to see the shock on the old ladies' faces, but after that it would just get ugly and more and more difficult for her, so she chose to give them nothing. 'That's very kind of you to say, Mrs Grigson.'

'Halley Campbell?' A young lady stood in the doorway that led to the consulting rooms. She wore an NHS ID badge at her waist and had a stethoscope draped around her neck.

This must be the locum she'd been booked in with.

'Excuse me,' she said to Mrs Grigson and her companion, smiling as she placed the magazine down, before walking away, glad to be out of the viper's pit.

The locum smiled. 'We're at the end of the corridor, I'm afraid.'

'That's fine. Gets me my steps for the day.'

The doctor opened the door to the consulting room and led her in. 'I'm Dr Meacham. Why don't you tell me what brought you in today?' She sat down by her desk and indicated the seat that Halley should sit in.

'Er…well, I'm not sure. I think I might be deficient in something. Maybe my iron levels? I'm so tired. Exhausted all the time and yesterday I nearly passed out in the village shop.'

Dr Meacham nodded. 'Okay, and how long have you been feeling like this?'

'I've not felt right for a few days, but I've been iron deficient before and it kind of feels like that.'

The doctor smiled. 'Well, as you're a temporary patient we don't have your medical records here for me to check.'

'Oh, that's right, yes. I had to fill in a form yesterday. Did my surgery not send over my files?'

'We don't appear to have them yet, I'm afraid. So, before when you felt like this, how did they treat it?'

'Iron pills for about three months, I think it was.'

'Okay, and otherwise, you're fit and well?'

'Yes.'

'No chance you could be pregnant?'

Halley smiled, thinking of the night she'd spent with Archer. They'd used a condom. 'No.'

'Okay. You're sure?'

'Absolutely.'

'Are you sexually active?'

She blushed. 'I have been, yes, but we used protection.'

'What kind? Are you on the pill?'

'No, we used a condom.'

'All right, and are you under any stress at the moment? Has anything changed in your life recently?'

'I'm here looking after my mother. She broke her hip, so I'm caring for her and helping run the farm.'

'That's a lot of work! No wonder you're tired. Okay, what we're going to do, if it's okay with you, is that I'll do a basic set of obs, then we'll get a sample of your blood to send off and see if you're deficient in anything at all. And we'll put in an hCG anyway, just in case, to make sure you're not pregnant because, even though protection is great, nothing is one hundred per cent effective, okay? How does that sound?'

'Fine. Could you do the bloods now? It's just a bit of a palaver if I have to come back for another appointment, what with looking after Mum and needing to be at the farm.'

'I'll do it now.'

Dr Meacham got out the equipment she would need and examined both of Halley's arms. 'Nothing obvious.'

'Yeah, people always struggle to get my blood.'

'Challenge accepted.' The doctor smiled, palpating her arms to find good veins. When she thought she'd got one, she stuck in the needle, but couldn't get anything out at all. She tried a second time. Still nothing. 'Huh. Maybe you were right. Let me see if one of the nurses is free.'

'Okay.'

Halley sat in the room on her own for a moment and then Dr Meacham reappeared, followed by Chloe, the nurse. A familiar face.

'This is Chloe. She's our nurse practitioner. She's going to have a try, is that all right?'

'Fine. Hi, Chlo, how are you doing?'

Chloe smiled at her. 'Not too bad. How are you? I'd heard you were back to look after your mum. How's that going?'

'Exhausting.'

Chloe nodded. 'I know the feeling. I'm doing the same thing.'

'Is your mum not very well?'

She grimaced. 'Parkinson's.'

'I'm sorry, that must be hard.'

'It is, but… I don't mind. It's my mum, you know?'

Halley nodded. She felt the same way. It had been hard to come back here, to a place she'd always wanted to escape from, but her mother had needed her and it was the right thing to do.

'Okay, so I won't stick unless I'm absolutely sure, because you've had two attempts already.'

Halley liked Chloe. She was pretty. Blonde-haired. She had a kind face. The kind of person you could imagine being wonderful with young kids, old-age pensioners and animals. If she were a cartoon character, bluebirds would encircle her and do her household chores.

'There you go.'

Halley looked down. Chloe had got the sample. She pressed a cotton-wool ball down in the crease of her elbow and asked Halley to press on it, before she applied a strip of tape.

'Thank you.'

'You're welcome. Maybe I'll see you around? Or we should get together and have a drink one day?'

'Sure. I'd like that.'

Chloe smiled and left the room.

'How long till I get the results?'

'A day or two. But in the meantime, I'm going to prescribe you some iron tablets, just in case. Take them every day, preferably with orange juice to help their absorption. We'll text the results to your phone—let me just check the number with you.' Dr Meacham read out the number she'd given them.

'Perfect.'

'And if anything comes back that's a little worrying, I'll give you a call.'

'Great. Thank you for seeing me.'

'No problem. In the meantime, look after yourself. Take frequent breaks, if you can, and make sure you're eating healthily.'

'Thank you, Dr Meacham. It was a pleasure to meet you.'

'You too.'

And Halley left the surgery feeling optimistic and bright. She had no doubt that it would come back as iron-deficiency anaemia, and she could take care of that with a pill every day. And then she could go back to feeling better and less tired.

And life could go back to normal.

Exactly as she liked it.

CHAPTER FOUR

I'm going up to Rookery Point again tomorrow night. Skies are meant to be clear. We should be able to see Jupiter.

HE TYPED OUT the message on his phone, his thumb hovering over 'Send'.

He felt it only fair to warn her that he would be there. Clearly she liked gazing at the stars too, and if she was going to go, he didn't want to just show up and make her think that he was stalking her or something. Telling her his intention ahead of time would absolve him of any blame and, worded like that, it didn't come across as an invitation.

Or did it?

We should be able to see Jupiter.

'We' meant stargazers in general. The world. Not the two of them. But he could see it might be ambiguous and she might take it the wrong way. He wasn't asking to see her again, or repeat what had happened the last time they were up on Rookery Point. Not that he'd say no, but...

Did you hear that Jupiter should be visible tomorrow night? I'm going up to Rookery Point to check it out.

He grimaced. It still sounded like an invitation. He deleted the message and typed another one.

Fair warning... I'm going to be at Rookery Point tomorrow night to see Jupiter.

Better. He pressed 'Send' and heard the whoop noise as the message got sent into the ether.

Fair warning—it sounded as if he was just giving her the heads up that he was going to be there, so that she could pick another place if she wanted to. He didn't need her there, whilst at the same time he was letting her know about Jupiter, in case she didn't know. Giving her a chance to see it, too. Though not with him.

Even if he would be happy to share that experience with her again. Even just sitting chatting to her might be nice. He'd enjoyed talking to her. She was easy to chat to. Easy on the eye, as well, and now that he knew her more intimately…

No. Stop it. That can't happen again. I will not allow myself to think anything more for Halley Campbell.

It was a dangerous road to walk down and if he did, he'd only get wrecked all over again. Halley was here temporarily. Her life was in Scotland these days. His was in Yorkshire. He had a business here! His entire life! Only being her friend was practical and logical.

And safer for everyone involved.

But to sit beneath the stars with her again would be…simply magical.

As a young boy he'd had all the various teenage-crush ideas. Kissing her. Holding her hand. Having everyone know that she was his girl and them being amazed.

Halley Campbell and Archer Forde? Are you kidding me?

All the other boys would be jealous and all the girls would be confused, because they'd think Halley could have had anyone. Why pick sad little Archer Forde?

He'd imagined having picnics with her, or walking by the river. He'd imagined one day getting down on one knee and proposing to her. She would gasp with surprise, or cry, but ultimately say yes and then he would pick her up and swing her around…

And the knowledge that that would never happen was sad, yes, but…he liked that things were different between them now. He wasn't the Archer Forde he used to be. He'd filled out. Grown. He wasn't a sad, pathetic figure any more. He was a businessman. A trained veterinary surgeon with a thriving practice. He'd once heard someone refer to him as Burndale's most eligible bachelor!

Now things were different. He and Halley were friends. She knew him. She would never forget him now. And they would always have that one, hot night.

Could he possibly ask for anything more?

As promised by the weatherman on TV, the skies were clear and Archer was settled on Rookery Point, with his telescope pointed at the sky, staring at Jupiter. After the moon and Venus, Jupiter was often the third brightest point at night and it looked beautiful. Looking at the planet always made him feel as if his issues, his problems in life, were so insignificant, when he thought about the vastness of the galaxy and the universe.

Human beings could get so caught up in

worrying about stuff that really they ought not to worry about! Did any of it matter? When you thought about the vastness of the cosmos? He sat back and sighed, lying down on the ground with his hands behind his head, enjoying the soft cool breeze and the sound of the trees rustling in the wind. He sensed a movement off to his left and turned to see a rabbit bolt out of sight and he smiled, then frowned as he saw headlights coming up the hill road towards Rookery Point.

Was it Halley after all?

Or was it some other stargazer?

Or maybe just someone looking for a quiet spot to park up?

It could be anyone and he didn't want to get his hopes up. If it *was* Halley, then what would that mean? That she was just here because it was the best place in Burndale to view Jupiter, or that she was here because she wanted to spend some more time with him? The latter would be good, but they'd both agreed they were only friends. Friends with benefits?

The vehicle stopped at the car park and he heard a car door open and then slam shut. Then footsteps. Quiet footsteps that crunched gently over gravel. Stopping briefly, as if the person was having second thoughts about continuing on, and then starting again.

The figure appeared from the shadows and he turned to say hello, not expecting he would be lucky enough to see Halley, only to see that it was, indeed, Halley.

A smile lit up his face, falling slightly only when he noticed that she didn't look happy at all. She looked upset. And she didn't have a telescope with her or anything, so she didn't look as if she was here to stare at planets in the solar system. So what was she here for? 'Hey, you okay?'

'No. No, I'm not okay.'

She seemed really upset. As if she was on the verge of crying. His concern for her washed over him like a wave. 'Is it your mum?'

Halley frowned and shook her head. 'No. No, it's not her.'

So if it wasn't her mum, then what was it? 'Come here. Take a seat.' He indicated the ground next to him, laying out his jacket so she didn't have to sit on the grass.

'I'll stand, thanks.'

'Okay.' So he stood, too. Waiting.

He saw her swallow. Saw her look around them. Down at his telescope. Up at the sky. Saw that she was gathering herself to tell him something that had to be momentous.

'Two days ago, in the shop after I...'

'After you got dizzy?'

She nodded. 'I…er…went to the doctor's. Just in case. I've been feeling…odd, lately, and she examined me and took bloods and all that jazz.'

'Okay.' He couldn't read her. She wouldn't look him in the eye. 'Oh, God, are you sick?' If she had something terrible, like cancer or anything, he wasn't sure he'd be able to bear it!

'No, I'm not sick, Archer. I'm pregnant. Pregnant with your baby and I know it's your baby because you're the only person I've had sex with in months! And yes, I know we used a condom, but those things are only like ninety-seven per cent effective and it looks like we are in that three per cent that it didn't work for.' Now she looked at him, to gauge *his* reaction.

Pregnant.

Pregnant!

He opened his mouth to say something, but nothing came out as the import of her words sank into him like punches. Pregnant. A baby. There was a baby. His baby. In Halley. They'd made a baby. Accidentally, but still. So what the hell were they meant to do?

'I don't know what to say.'

'Then that makes two of us. I just got the blood results back late this afternoon and I knew I had to tell you. I shouldn't have to struggle with this on my own.'

'No.'

Pregnant! What the hell were they going to do now? All these years he'd told himself he would not get into a serious relationship ever again and now he was going to be a father? Could there ever be a more important relationship in life? To parent a child?

'I don't know what to say.'

'You said that already.'

'I know! But…are you keeping it?'

'I don't know. I think so. I can't ever imagine having a… I don't know. This isn't a good time to be having a baby! I mean, I have the farm and Mum and my life back in Edinburgh and it's not like we're in a committed relationship and… I never planned on this happening! I've never wanted this!'

As she grew upset, he reached out and pulled her close, wrapping his arms around her, sharing her distress and confusion. They were both in the same boat here. 'We'll get through this together,' he muttered into her hair, not entirely sure how they would actually achieve that. Her hair smelt like flowers. How could they get through this together, if he couldn't concentrate when she stood so close?

'How?'

That's the million-dollar question, Halley.

'Somehow. We'll figure it out. We're grown-ups…we can handle this.'

'I don't want to be known as a failure in this village again, Archer. I can't be!'

'You're not going to fail. *We're* not going to fail.'

'That's easy for you to say. Society always looks down on women more than men. They'll see this as my fault. She couldn't find a guy to marry her in a church without discovering he's a lying bigamist and now look at her. Pregnant and alone. Couldn't even find a guy to be her baby's daddy!'

'Hey…you're not alone.'

'Aren't I?' She pulled away to look up at him. 'We're not in a relationship and I'll be the one left holding the baby and looking after it all the time, except on what? You'll have it weekends? What kind of life will that be?'

'We'll find a way to make it work.' He wasn't sure how at all. Halley's concerns were real and viable. If this went all the way and they weren't in a committed relationship, then how often would he get to see his child? How much would be enough? He'd never planned on becoming a father but, now that was a real possibility, he couldn't imagine not knowing his child! He'd grown up without his own father around and always promised himself he would never do that to a kid of his own.

'Look, we're both in shock. Let's take some time to let this settle in. Think about it. We're both just blindly reacting right now. We need time to absorb this news and then think about what we will do.'

'Well, the clock's ticking, Archer.' She stared at him.

He stared back. His gaze dropped once to her belly and then he was unable to look away.

It most certainly was.

Her mother was asleep when Halley got back from Rookery Point. She was glad of it, but knew she would have to tell her mum the news sooner rather than later.

Oh, God! I'm going to have to tell Hillary, too!

Hillary would no doubt laugh, or be smug. She'd always thought she was the better sister. The one that had done well for herself. The one who'd found a decent husband and had her babies in wedlock.

Hillary has twins. Twins! What if that runs in the family and I'm carrying two babies, as well?

Halley slipped into the kitchen and grabbed a biscuit to calm her stomach and nerves. Archer had taken the news better than she'd thought. He'd been pretty calm, though his eyes had looked panicked for a little while. She couldn't blame him. She felt the same way.

A baby!

As a little girl she'd often dreamed of finding her prince. Her knight on a white horse, who would make her swoon and fall in love. Who would place a ring on her finger and make her the happiest woman in the world. And she would bear his children and they would make everyone else jealous with how perfect their little family was.

She'd been in love with love. In love with the idea of a perfect romance. What little girl wasn't? And she'd been so sure that that ideal would fall into her lap one day.

It was why she'd made such a mistake with Piotr. Because their love story had been perfect. Too good to be true. A holiday romance that had become something deeper. Or so she'd thought. But Piotr had been a conman. A swindler. Who'd preyed on her naivety. But thank God she'd found out the truth before that ring ended up on her finger. Before she'd got pregnant with his child, because he'd mentioned that a lot. About how happy he would be to be a father and how they would start trying on their honeymoon. And she'd loved him so much she'd agreed to it!

Let's meet for coffee tomorrow. I have the afternoon free. Let me know a time that's good for you. Or I could come to the farm, if that's better. A x

She stared at the text. Appreciating that Archer hadn't run for the hills the second she'd told him, or offered to pay for an abortion, or anything like that. Of course they needed to talk about it. There was so much to discuss!

But even though this had never been in her plan, she knew, deep down, that she would be keeping this baby. Hopefully Burndale wouldn't notice she was carrying until she felt it was the right time to tell anyone and she and Archer could come to some arrangement regarding visiting. Because she had no idea where she was going to live now. Edinburgh had always been a bolt-hole, but she'd begun to hate it there and here there was family and…

Archer was here. The baby's father.

But he'd told her he didn't do relationships. That night on Rookery Point, the first night they'd met, he'd told her he wasn't looking for a serious relationship and never would be. He wanted to remain free to live his own life uncomplicated by anyone else's.

She'd naively said the same thing too, as if this were something they could control.

But life had a way of throwing a spanner in the works and if her life had to change?

Then so did his.

She'd agreed to meet him in the local café. He was glad of that. A public space, where neither of them could lose their composure. Where both of them would be civil. At first she'd argued against it. Not wanting to be seen in public with him, in case it got the gossip mill going anyway, but he reminded her that people were already discussing her near-fainting episode in the shop and they could explain their chat in the coffee shop as one person simply checking to make sure the other one was all right.

'The less we hide, the less they'll talk. Make this a big secret and we've no chance.'

Thankfully, she'd agreed.

He understood her reticence. She'd disappeared from Burndale after her wedding disaster, but he'd been here and he knew how the rumour mill had leapt into action. For *weeks*. People were discussing Halley for far too long and he'd hated it, on her behalf. And he'd experienced something similar when Amy had died and he'd endured weeks of pitying looks.

Gossip was a commodity in a place such as Burndale, where so little happened. It didn't have a high crime rate, the kids were mostly good, the only thing to talk about was each other and if that meant discussing something as simple as number sixty-seven putting in a new kitchen, or the local vet losing his girlfriend to brain cancer? They were both fair game.

He sat nursing a coffee and waited for her to arrive. He'd chosen a booth at the back, away from the window, that gave them the most privacy, and kept checking his watch as the time they'd agreed upon came and went.

Was she not going to show?

The bell above the door tinkled announcing a new arrival and he looked up and saw her come in, her eyes scanning the tables, until her gaze met his and she nodded, before heading over, sliding into the booth.

'Hey.'

'Hi. Can I get you anything? Tea? Coffee?'

'Tea, please, and maybe a slice of cake if they've got any?'

'Sweet tooth?'

'Nausea. Strangely, eating helps.'

'Oh. Right.' He got up and ordered for her,

choosing a slice of Madeira, which he thought would be the most plain, figuring she wouldn't want anything chocolatey or creamy. But then chose a slice of lemon meringue for himself, in case he was wrong and she'd want his instead.

Who knew?

He brought the tea and the cake over to the table and settled opposite her. 'There you go.'

'Thanks. That's perfect.'

He watched her add sugar and milk to her tea. Stir it. Take a sip. Then she looked up at him and sighed.

'So?'

'So…'

'Have you told anyone?' she asked in a low voice, looking around them.

'No. Have you?'

'I told Mum. Figured she'd need to know. She already wants to hire some extra lads from the village to *"take on the heavy lifting"*, just in case.' Halley did the speech quotes thing with her fingers. 'I'll tell Hillary later.'

He nodded. Thinking of Hillary in her swish car with leather seats, her power suits and her twin children. 'Do twins run in the family?'

Halley met his gaze and laughed. 'God, I hope not. Hills is the only one that I know, so maybe it was a freak occurrence or something? Why? Twins scare you?'

'Does it not scare you?'

'I'm *terrified*. One baby is a bombshell. Two of them?' She shook her head in wonder. 'Hills coped because she got a nanny in full time, but, even then, I still remember how she used to look in those early days. Exhausted. Confused. Sleep-deprived.'

'You can look that way with one,' he said, remembering how Axle had looked in the early days when he'd still been with Joanne.

'So what are we going to do? How are we going to manage this situation that we find ourselves in? I mean, it's hardly ideal, is it? We don't live together. We're not in a relationship. We hadn't planned this.'

No, it wasn't ideal. But that didn't mean they couldn't find a way to make it work. 'I'll be honest with you, Halley. I've never wanted kids, but I knew the second you told me that there was going to be one and that I was going to be a father—I knew instantly that I was never going to let my child feel the way I felt when I grew up.'

'And how was that?'

'Abandoned. Alone. Fatherless. A burden. I won't do that to my child. I'm going to be in its life as much as I can.'

'But how? You live here. Your business is here and my life is up in Scotland.'

'Then one of us agrees to move.'

She raised an eyebrow. 'I suppose you mean me? Come back here? To be gossip fodder? Halley Campbell? Single mother, as well as jilted bride?'

'You wouldn't be a single mother. We'll find a way to co-parent.'

Halley laughed. 'Oh, just what I always wanted.' She stabbed her fork into her Madeira and ate a bite.

'Well, then I'll move. I'll leave here. Find a veterinary posting in Edinburgh. Maybe locum for a while, if I have to.' He didn't want to. Not really. But this wasn't about just him any more. If he was going to become a father, then he was willing to make sacrifices. Compromises. And if Halley wanted to stay in Edinburgh, then he'd move there, too.

She stared at him. 'You'd do that for me?'

He shook his head. 'No. I'd do that for my baby.'

They were hardly the most romantic words she'd ever heard in her life, but romance wasn't what she was after here. He was offering to up sticks and move his life up north, to be with his child, so that they could parent this child together.

She was grateful for the offer.

'You don't have to do that.'

'But I will if I have to.'

'You don't.'

'But—'

'Archer, no. You don't have to move across the country to be up there when…when I'm not even sure if I'm happy up there anyway.'

'Oh.'

'I've hated Burndale. Believe me, I've hated this place and what it can do to you when you've been treated badly, but…up in Edinburgh hasn't been a picnic for me either.'

'How do you mean?'

'Anonymity is great for a while, but at the end of the day I sit in my flat and I'm all alone. I don't have family around me. I don't have any friends I've known my whole life and I can't imagine wanting to parent in a place where I don't have any support.'

'It takes a village.'

'What?' She frowned.

'It's what they say, isn't it? It takes a village to raise a child.'

She nodded. 'Perhaps they're right? That it's not something you can do alone. Well, you can, but it's going to be difficult for you. I fought coming back to Burndale so much, but maybe it's the right thing here. You'd still have your job and your brother and I'd have my family. The farm. Hills, for goodness' sake!'

'So…you're staying here? Is that what you're agreeing to?'

She nodded. 'I think I am.'

He let out a long breath. Smiled. 'Okay. So we've made a start. On deciding the best thing for our child. You see? We can do this. We can find a way.'

'Agreed.' She smiled. But she still felt sad inside. This wasn't what she'd imagined for herself when she was a little girl. She'd always imagined having a family and being happily married and in love with an amazing guy. Instead, she was getting this deal. Co-parenting. Agreeing to stay in Burndale, a place she'd always felt the need to run away from. Was she making a big mistake?

'You look sad, though.'

She smiled. Even though he was right. She felt sad. This wasn't the way life was supposed to happen! And even though Archer was a great guy, they were hardly in a relationship with great foundations, were they? They weren't madly in love, even if she did think he was hot. Damn it, he was probably the most eligible bachelor in the village! 'It's just not what I'd imagined for myself, that's all. I don't want to do things in life because I have to. I want to do them because I want to. Because I'd love to.'

'I get that. I kind of feel that way, too. Look, I know this is probably way out there and everything and we've barely discussed the basics, but why don't we agree to meet every day? Get to know one another a little more. We're going to raise a child together, so we need to know one another inside out.'

'And how do you propose we do that?'

'We meet. We talk. We share dinners or lunches. We get to know one another. I could introduce you to Axle.'

'Sounds like dating and I think we've established that neither of us wants that complication. It's complicated enough.'

'Then they won't be dates. Let's call them meetings. Strategic planning meetings.'

Halley laughed. 'Sounds like we might need a secretary to take the minutes.'

'We'll take our own minutes.' He reached across the table and took up her fingers in his. 'Let's get to know one another properly, Halley Campbell. Let's get this right for our child from the very beginning.'

It sounded like the best she could have hoped for. Archer seemed keen. He wasn't running away...he wasn't absolving himself of all responsibility. It sounded as if he cared a great deal as to how his child would feel and he wanted to be around. Could she have asked for a better reaction?

'Then why not come to mine for dinner tonight? Meet Mum and Hills. Become part of the family.'

He looked surprised.

'Too much?' she asked.

'No. No, it's not too much to ask. Fine. What time is dinner?'

She smiled. 'Our first strategic planning meeting will be at six p.m. How does that sound?'

He smiled and nodded. 'Then I second and carry that motion.'

CHAPTER FIVE

HE FELT NERVOUS about going around to Halley's for dinner with her mum and sister. He wasn't used to meeting parents and officially declaring himself in a relationship with someone, apart from Amy's parents, and even now it wasn't because he and Halley were in a romantic relationship.

This was something else.

They were going to bring a child into the world. Maybe it was still too soon to be announcing this to everyone, but he could understand Halley being scared by this and needing to tell people. She already had so much on her plate, what with the farm and looking after her mum. And now this bombshell that she'd probably stay in Burndale to live!

He had to admit to being incredibly happy that she wasn't going to be leaving and taking his child away! That would have been horrible for him to deal with. The guilt itself would be incredible. And the idea that he might have had to up sticks and go to Edinburgh had been worrying. Leave everything behind? Leave Axle? He and his brother were so close, he couldn't imagine not being able to just pop round to see him whenever he felt like it.

But if she was going to stay, then where would she live? On the farm? Or would she look for somewhere in the village?

He parked by the house, grabbed the bunch of flowers he'd bought at the shop on the way over and got out of his car, knocking on the front door.

Presently, the door opened and there stood Halley, smiling and looking at the flowers in wonder. 'Oh, they're beautiful! Thank you!'

He maintained his smile. 'Ah. This is awkward. They're actually for your mum.'

'Oh!' She laughed and stepped back. 'Not awkward at all. Come on in. Please excuse the mess. Everything's all over the place.'

'Don't worry about it.' He followed her down the small hall and into the living area. Sylvie was sitting in one of the armchairs, propped up with plenty of pillows.

'Excuse me if I don't get up, Archer,' Sylvie said, smiling at him warmly.

'How are you doing?' He leaned down to

drop a kiss on her cheek and presented her with the flowers.

'Oh, they're gorgeous, love! You shouldn't have!'

'My mum didn't teach me much, but I did learn that you never arrive at someone's house for a meal without taking some sort of gift.'

'Well, it's not me doing all the cooking. These flowers should be for Halley. She's doing all the work.'

'We'll both enjoy them,' Halley said, taking them from him. He watched her go into the kitchen and rummage in a cupboard for a vase, finding one and filling it with water.

'How are you getting along after your surgery?'

'Much better. A lot of the stiffness has gone and I've been given all this physio to do, but I should be more like myself soon.'

'She's trying to run before she can walk,' Halley called from the kitchen. 'I caught her trying to do the stairs earlier on her own.'

'I can do the stairs, love,' Sylvie insisted.

'But only if you've had your painkillers. Take a seat, Archer. Can I get you a drink?'

'Whatever you're having is fine. Hillary not here yet?'

'She's coming over later. Her court case has

run over time and she's stuck in traffic from Ripon.'

'Oh. Okay. Do you need any help in the kitchen?'

'Er… Can you rinse the rice for me?'

'Sure.'

He set to work in the kitchen, rinsing the uncooked rice in cold water first before it was cooked. 'Something smells good.'

'Chicken tagine. Ever had it?'

'I don't think I've ever had Moroccan food.'

'Then you're in for a treat,' Sylvie said. 'Halley's tagine is to die for.'

'Mum! You don't need to sell Archer on what a great little cook I am.'

'Don't I? He might want to know that the mother of his child can cook a decent meal.'

Archer paused. It was the first time someone other than he and Halley had referred to *their* baby. 'I'm sure the tagine will be great,' he replied diplomatically.

'Do you cook, Archer, love?' asked Halley's mum.

'I do. I love to cook, actually.'

'So you're not one of these men that lives on take-outs and meal deals?'

He smiled politely. 'No.'

'Good.'

Halley turned to him in the kitchen and mouthed the words *I'm sorry.*

'Hey, if this is the limit of the inquisition, then tonight is going to go just fine,' he whispered back.

'You'll be lucky.'

'What are you two whispering about?' Sylvie called.

'Cooking instructions, Mum!'

'Oh. Well, come in here when you have a spare moment. I think we have a lot more important things to talk about tonight.'

'She's right,' Archer said.

'Well, don't say that out loud. We'll never hear the end of it.'

He laughed. 'Anything else I can help with?'

'No. Now that the rice is on, we've got about eight minutes of interrogation. You ready?'

'Absolutely.'

'Okay, let's get this easy round done. Hills might be a lot worse.'

'So…a baby. That's a big life-change for the both of you.'

Halley gave Archer a small, supportive smile. 'Yes, it is.'

'How are you going to deal with it? Because if everything goes well, in a few months all our lives will change and I need to know if

I'm going to be on babysitting duty up in Edinburgh. Because if I am, I'll need to arrange someone permanent to manage the farm.'

Halley hadn't thought about how a baby arriving might affect her mum. 'I've decided that I'm most likely going to return to live in Burndale, Mum.'

'Really, love? I thought you couldn't wait to leave?'

'Well, things have changed, and Edinburgh is amazing in many ways and all, but it doesn't have family and I think I would like my child to know its family. Grandparents, aunts and uncles and all.'

'Oh. I suppose your mum feels the same way, Archer?'

Halley grimaced.

'I haven't told my mum about the baby yet.'

'Why not?'

'We're not that close.'

'That might change with a grandchild on the way.'

'She could barely be there for me, I don't think she's going to be all that interested, to be honest with you.'

'Well, I'm sorry to hear that,' her mum said. 'But I do like the idea of you coming back to Burndale, Halley. It's not been the same with you so far away and not seeing you very often. Have you looked for places? What sort of thing are you looking for?'

Halley shrugged. 'I don't know. I haven't looked at anything. I only pretty much decided today.'

'Will you be going back to Edinburgh to work your notice?'

'I don't know.'

Her mum nodded. 'Maybe you could help her look for a place, Archer?'

'Er, sure! When I'm not working, of course.'

'Fantastic. It is something you should decide together, because wherever she picks is going to be the place she raises your child, so you'll want somewhere nice and suitable.'

He nodded. 'Of course.'

Halley wondered if he was always this polite. Her mum was kind of leading this conversation for them. Maybe if they got it all out of the way now, when Hillary arrived there'd be nothing left to sort out! 'There's a lot for us to decide, Mum, we know that. We're still getting used to the idea that we might be parents. Give us some time.'

'God willing, everything will be fine, but, believe you me, I'm talking from experience and Hillary will say the same thing, but these next few months will go by so fast for you.

You need to make decisions and get everything in place sooner, rather than later.'

'You're right, Mrs Campbell.'

'Call me Sylvie, Archer.'

Dinner went well, even if Hillary didn't arrive until after they'd finished eating. The chicken tagine had settled in her stomach well, for which she was grateful. She'd found out to her cost that some things she craved just wouldn't stay down for that long, so Halley was always hesitant when she did eat. She made sure not to overload herself. Eating little and often seemed to be the key to fighting the nausea.

And Hillary was as judgmental as Halley had imagined she would be, grilling Archer over his intentions and making conversation difficult.

'This must be a shock for you, Archer? I don't know many eligible bachelors who take the news of fatherhood so calmly. Are you just making all the right noises to placate us?'

Archer had not looked away from Hillary. 'I'm making all the right noises because they are the right ones to make. Yes, this was a shock to us both and, no, it wasn't planned. But it is happening. and I think you'll find that I'm a man who takes responsibility for his actions. I'm going to be there for your sister and the baby.'

Hillary stared back at him, hard. 'You'll go to all the appointments? Have your name put on the birth certificate?'

'Absolutely.'

'You make the decision to be a father so easily, considering you told her that you never wanted kids. Didn't you do the same thing with Amy?'

Halley frowned.

So did Archer. 'That was different.'

'How so?'

'The situation was completely different. Amy was about to undergo cancer treatment. Her eggs would freeze better if they were fertilised.'

'But you'd not even discussed having kids with her at that point, had you? Her mum told me.'

Archer let out a low breath. 'I'm not on the stand, Hillary. You don't have to like me, but if you want to judge me, then judge me by my actions and my words as I present them to you. I am a good man, who is kind and considerate of people. No, I hadn't discussed having kids with Amy, but if she were to survive I wanted her to have that option in the future. But she died. I lost her and I thought I'd never have kids ever. But now there is going to be a baby. Our baby. And I am going to love it and be there for it, every single day. The second I'm not? You can stand before me then and tell the world "I told you so", but, believe you me, you will never get to say those words!'

Hillary didn't say much after that.

The evening drew to a natural close and Halley offered to walk Archer out to his car. She felt proud of him. Not many people were capable of standing up to her sister when she was in full flow, drilling them with questions. She kind of liked that Archer had silenced her. It was good. It meant that he was strong, as well as polite, and it had also kind of been a bit of a turn-on to hear him stand up for not only himself but the situation they both found themselves in.

'I'm sorry my sister was so rough.'

He smiled. 'That's okay. She was looking out for you. It's what siblings do.'

'Yes, well, she got her solicitor head on and drilled you like you were in court having sworn to tell the truth, the whole truth and nothing but the truth.'

'She's worried for you.'

'I'm worried for me. She just needs to support me. That's all I need from her.'

'They were both right, though. This time

will go fast and we need to know how we're going to do this. Finding a place for you to live, for example. I'll help, like I promised.'

She nodded. 'And I will inform my old job that I'm not coming back.'

'You're absolutely sure?'

'Yes. I am. They'll be fine about it. Then I'll just need to find something to do here. Any jobs at your place?' She laughed.

He shook his head, sadly. 'Not at the moment. But your mum's paying you for running the farm, right? You can keep doing that whilst you keep an eye out for veterinary nursing jobs.'

'I guess. Well, thank you for coming over and remaining graceful under my family's onslaught of questions.' She truly was grateful. Not many men would have done so. And strangely, sitting listening to him answer, she felt as though she could trust his answers, even though she hadn't known him that long. Because even though she didn't know him well, her mum did, and she'd know if he was lying about anything. She'd lived here all her life, same as him.

And Archer hadn't tried to evade anything. He'd even told them all about how strained the relationship was with his mum. And knowing that this situation wasn't something that he'd wanted, she was grateful and proud that he had sat there and answered every question as truthfully as he could.

He wanted to be there for the baby. That much was clear.

And knowing that she wouldn't be alone? Meant a great deal, indeed.

'You were great tonight.'

He met her gaze. 'So were you.'

'You think success is written in our stars?' she asked.

Archer looked up at the night sky above them. 'I hope so. I really hope so.' He pulled his gaze back to her. 'But I'd like to think that we both know how to keep our feet on the ground. And step one of that is finding you a place to live.'

She nodded. Her mum had offered to let her stay at the farm, but Halley was used to being independent now. She didn't want to take a step backwards and move back in with her mum. 'I'll get the local paper tomorrow. Start looking.'

'Make any viewing appointments for the weekend. I'll come with you.'

'All right. So we're doing this?'

'We are doing this.' He leaned in towards her and dropped a kiss on her cheek. His beard brushed against her cheek and she felt a surge of lust as she remembered that night on Rook-ery Point.

Did he linger? Was she imagining that? What she did know was that she yearned to feel his lips brush against her skin again.

And then he was sliding into the driver's seat and starting the engine. He wound down the window and gave her a little wave, before reversing out and then disappearing down the lane.

She watched his tail lights all the way, until they disappeared.

Was she being a fool for putting her trust in him? She'd thought she'd known Piotr and she'd been wrong. Was she relying too much on a man who'd told her at the very beginning of their relationship that he would never com-mit to another woman ever again?

Well, he's not committing to me. He's com-mitting to his child and that will have to be enough. It's not like I'm giving him my heart, either.

When he'd told Axle about his impending fa-therhood, his brother had been initially happy, then concerned when he'd learned that he and Halley were not in a relationship.

'I hope it goes well for you, Archie. Make

sure she knows your rights. Get your name on the birth certificate, everything.'

He'd promised he was going to do everything he could to stay in his child's life.

'And this Halley…she seems like she'll play fair with you? Give you access?'

'Yes.'

'I hope so, bro. For your sake, I hope so. I don't ever want you to go through what I am. You sure there isn't anything between the two of you? I mean, you hooked up to make a baby, there must be *something*.'

How could he tell Axle that this had been the girl of his dreams when he was younger? He'd just get excited and tell him to go for it and forget what happened before, but it was easier said than done.

Yes, he had feelings for Halley. How could he not? But it was so hard keeping them under control when clearly all Halley wanted was for him to be involved with their child. She'd not asked him for anything else, for any other type of commitment, and he understood why. She didn't want to be left behind again. She didn't want to be abandoned if anything went wrong. Why put herself through any more heartache? He got that. He didn't want heartache, either.

It was safer for the both of them if they kept this simple between them.

This was all for the baby.

He tried to keep telling himself that as he got ready to go and pick Halley up so they could drive around Burndale and look at the two properties that she'd arranged appointments for. Over the phone she'd told him the first property she'd found was a two-bedroomed flat above a shop. The second one was a small two-bedroomed cottage on the outskirts of the village. They both sounded fine and he was hoping that finding a place for her to have the baby in would be easy, because if they could cross something so major off the list, then they'd be well on their way. Once Halley had a place, they could move her in, get her settled, fix anything that needed fixing and then all she had to do was grow their child.

Simple.

But he couldn't help but feel that something was missing and he couldn't figure out what that was. He felt uneasy. Afraid. That no matter what he did to try and protect his child, he was somehow going to fail. He would somehow let it down, or hurt it, or be a bad father from the get-go and he couldn't allow himself to imagine how that might feel. He'd made a hell of a vow to Halley and her cautious sister, Hillary. And if he did make a mistake, if he wasn't the father he hoped he could be, would Halley do to him what Joanne had done to Axle?

When he knocked at the farm door, he heard Sylvie call from inside that the door was unlocked and to let himself in. He did so, uncertainly, calling out hello as soon as he stepped inside.

'She's upstairs in the bathroom, love. Morning sickness is bad today.'

He felt bad for her. 'Should I go see if she's all right?'

'I'm not sure she'd want to let you see her like that.'

'What caused it? Was it food, or…?'

'She put honey on her porridge and apparently that wasn't the best idea.'

'I'll go up. See if she needs any help.' He wanted to be there for her. He'd got her into this situation, after all. 'Is that okay?'

'Be my guest, then.'

He smiled at Sylvie and began to make his way up the stairs and followed the sounds of retching to a door. He knocked gently. 'Halley, you okay?'

There was a groan and then the flush of the toilet. 'Marvellous. Never felt better.'

The bathroom door opened and Halley stood there, looking pale and ashy. His heart melted in that moment, and he reached past her to the sink where there was a small basket of face flannels all rolled up. He took one, rinsed it under cold water and wrung it dry, before using it to pat her face.

She looked at him the entire time. 'Do I look a state?'

'You look beautiful.'

'You have to say that—I'm the mother of your child.'

'I don't say anything I don't mean. We don't have to do this today, if you're feeling rough.'

She laughed. 'Are you kidding me? I always start the morning this way. There's nothing that gets the blood pumping faster in the morning than twenty minutes' worth of retching before work.'

He put the flannel down on the side of the sink. 'You're okay?' She'd never looked more beautiful.

'I'm okay.' She smiled. 'Besides, if I'm going to be like this for a while, I can't put stuff off. We've got to get sorted. Time's a ticking.'

He nodded. 'Well, only if you're sure?'

'I'm sure, but thank you for trying to take care of me.'

In the small, confined space of the bathroom they were quite close. The proximity was disconcerting for Archer. He itched to reach up and tuck a strand of her golden hair behind her ear. He longed to touch her in some way. Just to let her know that he cared about her and that he didn't like that she was suffering with morning sickness. And perhaps he ought to say something? Because right now, standing here like this? Facing one another. Inches apart. Staring into her eyes? It was getting weird.

'I'm sure it will pass soon. When you get to three months, isn't that what they say?' It felt important to him to try and see the positives. Most pregnant women only suffered with this for a couple of months, even though he knew there were cases that lasted longer. Sometimes all the way to the day of delivery.

She nodded. 'Fingers crossed.'

The hopeful smile she gave him was sweet and he pushed down the urge to kiss her. Now was not the time, nor the place. And he wasn't sure if she'd give him a slap for trying.

The flat above the shop was situated over the local newsagent's. The door was at the back, in a small, cramped alley, and she looked at Archer in question. 'Think I'd be able to get a buggy through here?' There were large bins back here. One filled with cardboard, another filled with rubbish, and when the agent let them in, there was a narrow flight of stairs that took them up to the flat itself.

Halley tried to imagine herself coming back with a baby, having done a supermarket shop. 'Might be hard trying to get shopping and everything up these stairs. There's nowhere close to park my car, either, so if I had to carry a lot of stuff, back and forth, if I were on my own? I can't see how that would work.'

The agent, a young man from an estate agent that she didn't know, simply smiled. 'I believe the current owner arranges for a delivery from a supermarket and they carry it up into the flat for him.'

'Oh, I see.' She smiled, to be polite, as if the estate agent's answer were perfect and how had she not thought of that?

When the door to the flat was opened, they followed the agent inside. Archer wasn't saying much. She wondered what he was thinking. She needed a sign from him. Something.

'This room here, to the left, is the main living area with a front aspect that overlooks the village green.' The agent stood by the window and smiled as she and Archer stepped into the space. It was a decent-sized room. Painted white, with green curtains hanging. There was room for a three-seater sofa and another two-seater, a low coffee table and an entertainment unit. The TV was mounted on one wall. There wasn't much character to the place. It was just functional and so she tried to imagine sprucing the place up. Adding some colour. Her own furniture. Some plants. But then she'd also need room for baby stuff, too. What exactly did babies need? Judging by Hillary's house, they needed everything, but then she'd had to have double the amount what with having twins.

Oh, please don't let me be carrying twins.

A place for a cot, for sure. A Moses basket? A changing station? Though she guessed she could do that on a mat on the floor. Halley looked down at the current carpet and grimaced. It wasn't exactly in good condition. It looked old. Stained in places. It would need ripping out and replacing, which was going to add to any expense. Though she briefly wondered if there were any decent floorboards underneath it.

'Want to see the kitchen? The current owner has recently updated it and I think you'll find it's quite appealing.' The agent led them from the room and back into the hall. The next door on the left led to a small kitchen in bright white. It really was quite modern.

'There's not much surface space, is there?' The agent beamed. 'Not as it stands, but try to imagine it without that coffee machine taking up space, or the microwave. But there's plenty of storage.' He indicated the cupboards above by opening them and showing the interiors. 'And there's a concealed dishwasher just here.'

'Where's the washing machine?' Archer asked. 'Is there a separate utility room?'

'Er…no. I believe the owner uses a launderette in town.'

Archer raised an eyebrow at her. It told her everything he was thinking. That this place wasn't going to be suitable. Babies created a lot of laundry. She'd need a home with space for a washing machine!

'Let me show you the bathroom. Again, the owner has recently modernised it and, though there isn't a bath, there is a brand-new double shower, which is exquisitely tiled, if I do say so myself.'

Dutifully, they followed the agent around, though she strongly felt, and sensed Archer did too, that this place wasn't for them. The bathroom was fine and, yes, it had been done nicely, but it wasn't enough to sell it to her. The main bedroom was a fair size, but the second room was very small and certainly not big enough for all the things a baby would need. Halley wasn't an expert, but she knew this, at least.

'I'm not sure this is right for us,' Halley ventured.

'I agree with Halley. This isn't the one. Plus, it's above a newsagent's, so she'd be woken early every morning by the papers arriving.'

She'd not even thought of that. 'Can we go and view the cottage, instead?'

The agent clearly realised that this was not going to result in a sale. They had made up their minds. 'Of course. I'll meet you there in...' he checked his mobile phone '...half an hour?'

'Yes. Thank you.'

Halley and Archer headed back to the car and sank into the seats gratefully.

'How are you holding up? Do you need anything? Want to grab a coffee?'

'Ugh, coffee...you know what I really fancy?'

'What?'

'A strawberry milkshake. Extra thick.'

He laughed. 'Really?'

'The baby wants what it wants.'

'We'll pass by the café. Pick one up for you.'

'Great, thanks. I hope we have better luck with the next property. I'd viewed the photos of that flat online and it had all looked good.

It's amazing what they can hide with photography, huh?'

'I know. I think that flat will be good for someone without kids. Who's got some extra income to modernise the other rooms and replace the flooring and find some way to plumb in a washing machine, but it definitely wasn't right for us.'

'Us?' She looked at him and smiled.

'For you and the baby.' He smiled back and started the engine.

She'd known what he'd meant, but when he clarified his statement, *'for you and the baby'*, it made it seem as if she was on her own with this. That he was helping, but at the end of the day it would just be her and their child alone at home. Because he would get to drive away and leave them there. To carry on with the rest of his life.

Suddenly the extra-thick strawberry milkshake didn't feel all that appealing and so when he bounded out of the café carrying one and passed it to her, she could barely raise a smile of thanks.

They drove to the next property, the two-bed cottage on the edge of the village, but once again the details and the photography had been presented in such a way that just the sight of the property was disappointing before they'd even got inside. The only thing nice about it was the small garden out front. Neat lawns with a couple of shrubs. But the garden itself backed onto the road that edged their village and they both knew that traffic could be fast there, barrelling down the lane at high speeds. That wouldn't be safe for a young child. Not safe at all.

Once again, the estate agent did his best to try and sell them on the positives—a large cottage kitchen, an inglenook fireplace, a traditional range in the kitchen and two large bedrooms. But nothing could overshadow the facts that there was a large fishpond in the rear garden, damp climbing up the walls in the outhouse attached to the cottage and the property was single-glazed throughout and had a thatched roof that would need replacing within the next year.

It was all too much. Halley and the baby would need a place that was ready to move into. That needed the minimum of work doing to it, so that she could settle in with her growing bump and happily wait for her baby to be born, without worrying if the damp was getting worse, or if the roof was going to have to come off and be replaced.

The estate agent gave them his card and told

them to ring him if they had any questions and he sped away in his car.

Halley turned to Archer. 'I think this is going to be harder than we realised.'

'Yeah, stressful too. But, you know, that's just a couple of places, there's bound to be others and we still have time.'

She nodded and took a swallow of her milkshake. It had melted slightly, but tasted wonderful, settling in her poor, troubled stomach nicely. 'Well, thanks for coming with me.'

'I wouldn't have it any other way. Want me to drive you home?'

No. She didn't. Not yet. Despite the disappointing properties, she'd enjoyed being out and about with him and there was nothing pressing at home. Hillary was there looking after Mum. 'Could you not? I just want to… I don't know, have a break. Can we do that, or do you have to get back, or…?'

'It's no problem. Where do you want to go?'

She shrugged. 'Somewhere nice. Where we don't have to think about houses, or the fact that I'm pregnant and my life is about to change big time. I just want to be normal. I just want to not have to think. Is that okay? Know any place like that?'

He smiled as he gazed at her. 'I think that I do. There's a place that I go when I want peace and quiet and calm and I think it will be perfect.'

'Where is it?'

'You'll see it when we get there,' he answered enigmatically, starting the engine.

Halley smiled. She liked that he was keeping it a mystery. She liked that he was willing to spend time with her. That he wanted to help her find some peace.

He was a good man. He was being a good man. Had one been here, right before her eyes, ever since she was a little girl and she hadn't noticed? And she hadn't noticed because back when she was younger she'd been incredibly shallow and only noticed the boys who were captains of the rugby team. Boys who got the lead in school plays. Boys who had the most friends and were deemed cool.

She'd certainly not paid any heed to the guy who had sat quietly on the sidelines and watched her dissect a frog. That boy, back then, had seemed small. Weedy. Pale. He'd worn glasses that weren't trendy and, if she remembered correctly, he'd always seemed a bit…scruffy. A bit neglected. Which of course he had been. He'd told her so. And that just made her feel incredibly guilty. Because he didn't look that way now, and now she noticed him.

'Did I ignore you?'

He glanced over at her. Frowned. 'What?'

'At school? Was I even worse than that? Was I mean?'

'No! No, you were…perfect. You were… amazing.'

'I didn't speak to you. I didn't notice you.'

'Who did? Look, don't beat yourself up about something that happened when we were kids. It's a different life. You have different rules for yourself. In school, you do your best to be like everyone else. To fit in. To be the same. It's only when you're an adult do you realise how important it is to just be you and, no, you may not have noticed me, but you weren't mean. You were still you.'

'I think you're just being gracious and kind.'

He laughed. 'Well, that's me.'

'You're sweet. I should have noticed that, at least.'

'It's a bit hard to notice when I hardly spoke as you wielded a scalpel.'

'I should have noticed you, Archer. I should have made the attempt to get to know you.'

'Do you notice me now?' They had stopped at a red light and he was looking at her intently.

He was gorgeous. Manly. Cool and a little edgy. Intelligent and kind and he was going to be the father to her baby. In her life, for the rest of eternity, in some capacity. 'I do. Very much so and I'm glad of it,' she answered earnestly.

'Then everything worked out well, didn't it?'

Archer parked up in a car park near Ripon high street and led her to what looked, on the outside, like a normal run-of-the-mill book-shop called Many Worlds.

'Books?'

'And cake. Lots and lots of cake. Come on!' He was smiling. Happy as he pulled open the door and she stepped inside, straight into a magical mystery world, unlike any bookstore she had ever been in.

The interior looked like a forest and all the shelves were branches of trees, lined with books. But there wasn't any women's fiction here. No romance. No crime. All the books were fantasy, or science fiction or even hor-ror. There were nooks to sit and read, filled with comfy chairs or bean bags. There were models and figurines of creatures that looked like dragons and elves or swamp monsters. In one corner, there was a huge screen, playing the latest fantasy blockbuster with a group of people sitting in front of it, watching intently.

She turned to look at Archer, surprised. 'Tell me the truth. Are you a secret geek?'

He smiled. 'I am. And our child will be too, so get used to it. I shall introduce him or her to the possibilities of dragons, vampires, were-wolves and wizards. So get used to the idea right now.'

She laughed. 'I don't have to!'

He raised an eyebrow. 'Are you going to fight me on this?'

'Why would I? When I'm a geek, too? I love this place!' And she walked forward to a shelf lined with dark books, saturated with reds and purples and gothic fonts. They gleamed. They glowed. The typography was gorgeous, the artwork striking, drawing her in, making her slide one book out from the shelf after another, to read the blurbs on the back. Her pregnancy was forgotten. House-hunting forgotten. Feeling bad about her schooldays was over. Just being here, in this wonderful place, this magical world, was more than she could ever have hoped for! 'How didn't I know of this place?'

'You've been away. It opened up three years ago now, I believe. There's an upstairs you haven't seen yet, it's like a treehouse, with even more books and a café, filled with cakes and delicious pastries that you just know you shouldn't eat, but have to, because they look so amazing.'

She beamed a happy smile, feeling hungry for a change. 'We'll get up there in a moment. I want a proper look down here first. Ooh, that looks good!' She reached for a book. A thick one, a good five hundred pages, with a metallic green serpent on the cover, wrapped in and around the letters of the title, written in gold.

I could spend a fortune in here!

They passed a section that was all graphic novels and, though she'd never read one in her life, seeing them all face out like that intrigued her and she went in to browse them, picking up one or two that sounded interesting.

'You big into those?' Archer asked, smiling at her, enjoying her joy.

'Never read one in my life.'

He laughed and she liked the sound.

She smiled at him, noticing that he'd picked up a couple of books that he was carrying around, too. 'Show me.'

He'd picked up a book that was the third one in a trilogy that he'd been reading about a demon horde and the other title was a standalone that looked like a gothic thriller, judging by the creepy house on the cover. 'You can borrow them, if you like?'

'Thanks. I just might.' So they both liked

stargazing. Both loved animals and caring for them. Were both into fantasy and horror novels. And were both scared about getting into a full-time relationship. What else were they matching on? Apart from the fact that they were going to bring a child into the world together.

Maybe this could work? Maybe they were more similar than they realised? If they had the same beliefs and the same likes…then why couldn't this work out?

But as soon as she allowed herself to hope about the possibility, she instantly got scared. Because what if it all went wrong? In front of the whole village yet again? Imagine if they got together and set up a home together and had their baby and then it all fell apart? What would people say then? Could she fail in front of them again? Could she fail herself? She'd set herself these rules for a reason—to keep herself safe—and if she stuck to them and stuck to them hard, then she wouldn't be in danger at all, would she?

'Ready to see upstairs?' He proffered his hand.

She took it. 'Sure.'

There was an escalator that took them to the next floor and as they rose, they passed a tremendous mural on the wall of a castle perched high on a mountaintop and all around in the sky and sitting on the castle turrets were dragons of all colours and sizes. There was a dark forest and, if she looked carefully, as they rose higher and higher she saw little candle lights in the darkness and sitting around them were elves and goblins and pixies. All the things that made her heart sing. 'I think I know how I want to decorate the nursery,' she said, turning to smile at him standing behind her.

Archer laughed. 'Absolutely.'

When they reached the top, the smell of coffee and cake reached her nostrils, making her salivate.

The bookshop café was perfect. Lit by wall sconces as if you'd reached the top of the tower, the walls were painted grey and had all these nooks and crannies built into them and in each one lurked a creature, backlit by a glowing coloured light. The floor was painted as if it were exposed wood and in the gaps between the wooden slats you could see a magical land far below, through the clouds.

There were more bookshelves, filled with books that were highlighted as the bookseller's choice of the week, or there was a table with a large pile listed as being written by a local author. Each of them adorned with a golden sticker that indicated it was a signed copy. On one wall was a large glass case, filled with cakes and pastries, just as promised. It was a delight for the eyes, as well as the nose, and Halley had difficulty choosing what she wanted. In the end she went for a cake called the Dragon's Eye—a coconut macaroon with a pool of yellow jelly in the centre.

'This is amazing,' she said as they sat at a table. 'This was perfect. Just what I needed.'

'I did think about taking you to the observatory, but it's best to prebook.'

'That would have been amazing, too. Mum's going to be annoyed that I've bought a load of books, instead of buying a place to live, but…'

'You're allowed to treat yourself. And you're still you, with your own identity. You don't lose that just because you've become a mother.'

'Or a father,' she said. 'Do you think that'll happen? That we'll lose who we are?'

'I hope not.'

'Hillary talks about her children all the time. Them or her work. I'm not sure I know who she is any more.'

'She's your sister. She always will be.'

'I know, but she used to be into music big time. She could sing, you know? She had this amazing voice and I used to tell her to go on one of those TV shows and audition, because she'd be able to make it through, but I don't even hear her sing any more. Will we lose this? This interest in reading fantasy? Or not have the time to do what we love? Will we lose our interest in looking up at the stars? Will we lose ourselves when we become Mum and Dad?'

'I'll make sure that we don't. I'll ensure that we make time to each do our own thing.'

'How though? How are we going to do that? You'll live in your place. I'll live in mine. You'll be working. I'll be raising the baby. We could get lost in all of that.'

'We'll find a way.' He looked determined.

'You keep saying that, but *how*? You make all these promises and they're great, they really are, but when reality hits?'

'You think I'm not going to stay committed?'

'No. But I think we'll be separate. I'll have the baby most of the time, then you'll come over to pick up the baby to have for the weekend or whatever and you'll go off and do that alone and I'll be alone waiting for the baby to come back and...' She shrugged. 'That's not how I want this to be.'

'What do you want?' he asked softly, leaning forward, his eyes intense in the darkness of the café. She wanted to stare into his eyes for evermore. She wanted to lean forward and kiss him and taste him once again to remind herself that this was real. That he was real. That she was safe.

She wanted a relationship. She wanted them to have an equal share. She wanted to be a person in a loving and committed relationship if she was going to have a child. Not someone who treated their child like a timeshare apartment. But she was afraid to say it. Afraid to say what she really wanted, because if she did? And that wasn't what he wanted? Where would that leave her? 'I don't know,' she said softly, knowing that she was lying, but fear held her back from the truth.

She liked Archer. She thought that he was one of the good guys. He'd already shown her that he truly cared and would help her out as much as he could. But did he want love? Could he ever love again?

'Tell me about Amy.'

Archer blinked. 'What? Where did that come from?'

'Hillary brought it up—I thought we should talk about it. It's a significant part of your past.'

He looked about them and she could see he was trying to work out how he was going to tell this story. 'Amy was my girlfriend. She didn't come from Burndale. She was from Yorkshire, though. Worked as a drug rep and came into the surgery one day to argue with me about what the best anti-inflammatory was. I thought she was cheeky. Daring. She had this smile that brightened up the room, so I asked her for a drink and our relationship developed from there.'

'You loved her?'

Archer grimaced. 'I don't know. Probably. I was infatuated with her. She reminded me of...' He laughed. 'She knew her own mind. Knew what she wanted from life. Marriage and kids, the whole shebang. I wasn't ready. I wasn't sure I wanted to fully commit and then we found out that the headaches she'd been having a lot of were actually caused by a brain tumour.'

'Cancer?'

He nodded. 'A glioma. She was scheduled for chemotherapy, but because of her age they suggested that beforehand she use drugs to make her ovaries create a lot of eggs so they could be frozen for when she was better. The doctors said that the eggs would stand a better chance if they were fertilised and, because I was her boyfriend, her family turned to me.'

'What did you do?'

'What was I supposed to do? I couldn't walk

away. So I did what I had to do and they managed to freeze four healthy embryos. But Amy didn't respond to the chemotherapy. Nor the radiation. Her cancer was fast and aggressive and she died.'

'I'm so sorry.'

'Her family grieved, but after a time they got this idea that they could use the embryos in a surrogate, so they could still have a piece of their daughter. I think this is what Hillary was referring to. I didn't know what to do. What to say. I couldn't imagine it. I'd fertilised those eggs to give Amy a future, but she wasn't there any more and I'd been left in a difficult situation. I didn't want to have a child like that. Out in the world, without me. But thankfully, they changed their minds.'

'Really?'

He nodded. 'They were planning on leaving Yorkshire, emigrating to Australia, and they wanted to take the embryos with them, but I didn't give consent for them to do that. I didn't want a child of mine being raised halfway around the world with no contact and I also didn't think they should have pushed to have grandchildren, just so they could somehow hold onto Amy. That's not what she would have wanted and, in the end, they agreed with me.'

'Did you ever want a child?'

'Honestly? I never envisaged it. But it's happening and it's here. It's not me and Amy, it's me and you and we're a whole different kettle of fish. You're staying here in Burndale. We're going to be close and I'm going to be damned sure that I'm in the life of my child, so that it knows it has a loving father, who will be there for it, for the rest of its days.'

He paused. 'Listen…my childhood wasn't the greatest. I had no father. My mother was distant and unwell. I was made to feel like a burden and I swore I would never let any child of mine, if I had them, feel the same way. That's why I was against the idea of kids. But because my childhood was rubbish, doesn't mean my baby's childhood will be the same way. Children give us the opportunity to be better. To not repeat the same mistakes. Babies are a clean slate. A fresh start. A chance for us to be different, so that history doesn't repeat itself. I'm not going to let history repeat, Halley. I'm going to be present. I'm going to be loving. I'm going to be the best dad I can be, because my child deserves more than what I had.'

She could see the passion in his eyes. He meant every word and she reached for his hand without thinking. And that soothed her soul for a little while.

Archer Forde would not leave her to deal with this alone.

He would find a way to make this work.

She believed in him.

She believed in *them*.

CHAPTER SIX

HE WAS GLAD the subject came up. He was glad that she'd raised it, that Hillary had raised it at the dinner, too, because he'd not wanted to hide it and hadn't been able to think of a way in which to explain what had happened.

How could he have raised that? How could he have just dropped that into conversation? He'd never intended to have a family with Amy. She was fun. She'd been great. But had he ever viewed her as someone he wanted to be with for ever? And fertilising her eggs had been something he'd felt he had to do. He'd cared for her deeply and he'd wanted her to have the opportunity to have children in the future, in case her cancer treatment left her infertile, and embryos froze better than eggs.

He'd never thought she would die. He'd never thought she would be infertile, after the treatment, that was just something they warned you about as a possibility. And there *had been* a chance that he and she could work out. That they'd be together for ever. Nothing else had been on the horizon for him, so he'd thought he could make it work. He'd believed she'd get better. He'd been optimistic still, back then.

Losing Amy had been hard. One of the most difficult things he'd ever had to go through. Allowing himself to get attached, to develop feelings for her, to believe that he might have kids, that his future was more than likely tied into hers, had only made everything hurt the more when she'd died. Having hope taken away had been just as difficult to deal with as her death. He'd had to say goodbye to that idea.

Archer had thought that his mother's inability to love him and Axle had been horrible. To not have the love of someone who should love you… To have spent years craving his mother's favour… For her to just one time tell him that he was a good boy, that she was proud… He'd got used to yearning for love and so it had been easy to turn his affections to Halley at school and yearn for her from afar. She'd become his idea of perfection. He'd decided that if she ever were with him, then their love would be perfect. But he'd never been brave enough to speak up. To stand close. To engage with her, because he'd been too afraid of her rejecting him, too. Worse than that, what if she'd laughed at him? It was bad enough his own mother couldn't love him properly, if Halley rejected him as well, then his one iota of happiness that he nurtured secretly in his heart would die.

To lose a love he'd actually pursued? He'd got brave with Amy. She'd seemed safe. Less likely to hurt him. She was a love that he had allowed to creep in and wrap its tendrils around his heart and when those connections had broken apart with her death, those tendrils had torn him in two. Losing Amy had hurt so badly that he'd vowed to never love deeply again. Just so he never had to face such terrible pain again. Living in a state of numbness worked better.

But now there was Halley.

Now there was the baby.

And he knew he would fall in love with this baby and that would put him at risk for ever. What if it got hurt? What if it got sick, like Amy? Something serious? What if they lost it before it even got born? He couldn't imagine how that would feel.

As he drove her home, he must have been quiet in the car.

'Everything okay? You haven't said much.'

He smiled to reassure her. 'Just thinking.'

'What about?'

'Life. How you're never in control of it, even though you think you are.'

'Tell me about it.' She rubbed at her belly.

'Do you need anything?' He wanted to help her. Wanted to give her anything that she might need. If he could be her person strongly enough, then maybe he might feel a smidgen of what he needed himself.

She sighed. 'I need lots of things. I'm never going to get them though.'

He smiled, indicating to take the left turn that would take them back to the farm. As he drove towards it, he wondered if it would always be like this. Him spending a few hours with her, but then both of them going back to their own homes. Together, but *not* together. It would be the same when the baby was here. How much of his child's life would he miss because they didn't live together? Would he miss his baby's first word? The first time it sat up? The first time it slept through the night? Suddenly, he knew he couldn't live like that. He couldn't live another life missing out on the love he would feel for his child.

'I don't want to miss anything, Halley.'

'What?'

'I don't want to miss anything. I want to

be there for the milestones. The first nappy change. The first solids. The first sleeping through the night. I want to have to pace the floor of the nursery because the baby won't settle. I want to complain of being sleep-deprived. I want to be there for everything.'

She didn't say anything. If anything, she frowned, as if trying to think. Trying to find a solution.

'Maybe you should move in with me?' The words were out of his mouth before he could even think about what he was saying.

'What?'

'Maybe you should move in with me? When your mum is better and up and about and able to do things again. I have a nice three-bedroomed cottage. It's double-glazed, it doesn't have damp, there's no pool or pond in the back garden. I use one room as an office, but we could make that your room, so you have your own space, but we'd be together. We'd share everything equally. The garden is mostly lawn, so plenty of places to put up a Wendy house or a treehouse or whatever our kid wants. I have a washing machine. All mod cons. We could each be who we need to be, but, most importantly, we'd be there for our baby together.'

She stared at him in mute shock and surprise.

It was a crazy suggestion, he knew, but one that seemed to make sense. He had the room, and this way he could be there for everything and so could she. Neither of them would have to miss a thing.

'You mean that?' she asked after an inordinately uncomfortable amount of time.

'I do. It might be a little unconventional, but we could make it work. We get along. We like a lot of the same things, but this way we'd each still have our independence, whilst at the same time share the responsibility and care. Do you really want to be a part-time parent, Halley? Because I don't want to be. If I'm having a baby, then I want to be there for it. Always.'

She let out a laugh. 'It's a crazy idea!'

No. He didn't want her to think it was crazy. Or that he was joking. He meant this. 'Just think about it. I think it could work.' He pulled up at the farm and watched as she pushed open the door and got out. The soft breeze whipped at her hair, drifting across her face, and she had to tuck it behind her ear.

She stood there for a moment. 'When would you want this to happen?'

'Before the baby's born. That gives your mum plenty of time to recover.'

'But if we lived together, don't you think

that might be a little weird? I mean…what if you wanted to go out on a date?'

He frowned. 'I don't think either of us is going to have much time to go out on dates.'

Halley laughed. 'Maybe not. Hmm… Let me think about it, okay?'

'Okay, but just promise me you'll consider it carefully. I really think this could be the answer to our worries.'

She nodded. 'I promise.'

'Okay. I'll call you tomorrow.'

When she got in, her mum was halfway up the stairs.

'What are you doing?' She rushed over to help her sit back down onto the chair.

'My physio exercises! I need to do them at least three times a day.'

'But only when I'm home! What if you'd fallen over? Where's Hillary?'

'One of the lads said he thought that one of the pygmy goats was in labour, so she went out to check. She's been gone for some time, so I can only guess we have kids on the way. Or already here.' She sighed as she sat back in the chair. 'How did the house-hunting go?'

'Not great. Neither property was suitable.'

'Oh. Well, that's a shame. You were out for

some time, though. Did you go on to some-where nice?'

'A bookshop in Ripon.' She pointed at the bag she'd placed on the table. 'Archer bought me some books.'

'And what did he think to your choice in reading material?'

She smiled. 'Actually, Mum, he likes the same things.'

'Really? Well, that's interesting.'

'Why?'

'I don't know…it's just two young attractive people like yourselves, both into animals, both into astronomy, both into elves and magic… having a baby together. It's just surprising that neither of you can see what's right in front of you.'

Halley tilted her head to one side. 'And what is that exactly?'

'That you're perfect for one another.'

'I think it takes more than stars and magic to make two people fall in love, Mum.'

Her mum smiled her knowing smile. 'Oh, I don't know about that. I think stars and magic are just perfect.'

'Do you want some tea?'

'That'd be lovely, thanks.'

As Halley brewed a cuppa in the kitchen, her mind whirled with Archer's suggestion about moving in with him. About Mum's comments about how similar she and Archer were. How suited they were for each other. 'Mum… how did you know that Dad was the right man for you? How did you know he was the person you wanted to live the rest of your life with?'

Her mum looked at her oddly. 'Well, he was so lovely. So kind and thoughtful. He was always looking out for me. Always trying to make me smile or laugh. I just knew he would make a good husband. A good father.'

'And when he asked you to marry him, was there any hesitation?'

'None at all. I couldn't imagine saying no. Why? Has Archer asked you to marry him, love?' she asked, her voice rising in surprise.

'No! No, he hasn't. But he has suggested we live together at his place. He's a great guy, but I have all these reservations. Whereas with Piotr I had none, and look how that turned out!'

'You were very young when you met Piotr. Just turned twenty. You've had more life experience now. You know how things hurt, of course you're having reservations.'

'It's not love, or anything. He simply suggested it for the practical arrangements. He really wants to be there for his baby and not miss anything and he has a three-bedroomed cottage, so I'd have my own room.'

'I see. What's your gut reaction?'

'If he wants a relationship with his baby, then it's perfect. But if I move into his place, will I lose my own autonomy? Will everything be his rules because it's his place?'

'If you're worried about that, agree to it only on certain conditions, then.'

'I guess…'

'What sort of rules do you want in place?'

'I don't know. He's only just asked me as he was dropping me off. I haven't had time to think about it. It was such a surprise.'

'I've known Archer a long time, Halley. He's been coming here and caring for the farm animals for many years. He's been through a lot himself. He lost the love of his life, too. You're not the only one hurting here. I'd also bet you're not the only one feeling cautious and wanting to establish some ground rules. But he's a good guy, so just talk to him. Talk about what he's suggested and see if it could work.'

'He says we wouldn't have to do it until you were back on your feet again.'

'Considerate, see? But I'm getting stronger every day. I can manage the stairs. Slowly, but I can manage. And I'm walking more. You girls don't need to hover over me so much.'

'So you think I should do it?'

'I can't make that decision for you. But if you're not able to find a suitable place before the baby is born, it might just be the answer to your prayers. He's offered you your own space, so he's not presuming anything about the relationship.'

'No, he's not.'

Her mum looked at her strangely. 'Do you want something more from him?'

Halley met her gaze. 'I like him. I do. A lot. But I'm scared to think that anything could happen between us. And if we're in a forced proximity… I just don't want to make a huge mistake.'

'Moving in and allowing yourself to fall in love in case it all goes wrong?'

She nodded.

'You can't live like that, love. Look at how long you've been on your own. How happy have you truly been?'

'I've been fine!'

'But what if you could be more than fine?'

Halley didn't have an answer.

Archer's next patient was Sanjay Singh, bringing in his cat, Jess, because it had been injured during a fight with another cat.

Jess was a beautiful Siamese cat, chocolate

point, long and slender, but had a nasty bite mark on its side that looked as if it was turning into a bit of an abscess.

'Neighbourhood cat?' Archer asked.

'No. This was our fault. We went to the cat rescue place. My wife has always wanted to rescue an older cat and so we went and picked up this old codger. Big fella he is. Called Badger. We brought him in a couple of weeks ago. Saw Max. Just to get him checked over, you know? We tried doing slow introductions—you know, the way you're meant to—but then one of the kids left a door open and there was this big fight and this happened.'

'How did Badger come out of it?'

'Not a scratch. But he's this big fluffy Persian cat and I think his fur protected him from Jess's claws and teeth.'

'Lucky guy. Okay, Jess, let's have a proper look at this, shall we?'

He gave Jess a thorough examination, finding a couple of clean scratches on her ears and beneath her eye. The bite on the neck and shoulder area seemed to be the worst of it and he had to shave off some of her fur to get a decent look at the abscess that was forming. Her temperature was slightly raised, indicating the infection. 'Okay, so what we need to do is give Jess some antibiotics to help rid her of the infection. I could give her a painkiller as well, if you wanted, but she seems to be moving pretty well and isn't restricted in her movements. You say she's getting around the house normally?'

'Yes. Jumping all over the place. Getting on top of the fridge. My wife hates that.'

'Eating and drinking normally?'

'Yeah…yeah.'

'Toileting okay?'

'I think so. But she goes outside, so I can't be sure.'

'And she's washing and cleaning herself normally?'

'Yeah.'

'Okay. Well, I'll give you the meds and see how she goes. But if you have any concerns or anything, then just give the reception team a bell and we'll fit you in.'

'Okay, great, thanks.'

He waved Sanjay and Jess goodbye and in-putted the consultation into the computer. Un-fortunately cat bites were something he saw a lot in his job. Introducing two animals that didn't know each other into the same space was always going to be fraught with problems, especially if they were two adult cats that had already lived a bit of life. Were stuck in their ways and knew how they wanted their life to be. He supposed there were teething problems with anyone moving in together.

Would he and Halley have issues if she took him up on his offer to move into his place?

Part of him still couldn't believe he'd even asked it out loud! Another part of him told him it was the most sensible solution to all their problems. They were struggling to find Halley a place. It made simple economic and emotional sense. It would be beneficial to both their finances. They'd both be there to raise their child. They'd be able to make decisions together and they could each still live their own life.

It was sensible. And if they established ground rules between them, as well, so they each knew the other's expectations and limitations...then he couldn't see any reason why it wouldn't work.

Of course, it would be strange to actually live with Halley. He'd never lived with another woman before. He and Amy had been going out, but they'd not moved in together ever, even if he had felt as if he'd slept over a lot when she'd had chemo and he'd wanted to be there for her, in case she'd needed help in the night. But he'd still had his own place. His own bolt-hole. His own escape, for when it all became too much. That was why he'd told Halley they'd each have their own space. Their own room. They'd need that, because if she accepted, both their lives would be pretty much full on. And he felt sure he'd be able to separate his emotions if this happened. Liking Halley and loving Halley, living under the same roof…with rules in place, there was no chance he'd do something silly and risk it all.

Would he?

Because he knew he could never take that chance and ruin everything. He needed to be there for his kid and that was a strong enough reason not to risk pursuing anything physical or emotional with her.

A quick knock on his door behind him and Jenny, his new partner, popped her head in. 'Ready for a cuppa?'

He nodded. 'Absolutely! Sounds a great idea. I think we've got some chocolate biscuits lurking in the staff room, too.'

Halley had been scanning estate agents' websites and there simply wasn't anything suitable that came up. The only property that did was way out of her price range and so Archer's suggestion was seeming a more sensible idea with every second that passed.

When Archer texted to see how she was doing that morning, she sent him a text back and asked if she could meet him midday for lunch and a chat.

He suggested twelve-thirty in the village and she agreed to meet him then, saying she'd bring lunch and she'd meet him outside in the car.

When lunchtime rolled around, she saw him stride out of his practice and towards her car, giving her a quick wave.

She smiled in return and admired him as he grew closer. He really was a very attractive man and she almost had to pinch herself to tell herself that this was real. She was having a baby with this man!

'Hi. How are you doing?' He got in the car and leaned in to drop a peck on her cheek in greeting. She tried to ignore the fluttering of her heart and instead smiled and passed him a container.

'Great. Haslet and pickle sandwiches. That all right?'

He raised an eyebrow. 'Craving food?'

She laughed. 'Craving food. We can stop off and get you something different, if you'd like?'

'No, it'll be fine. Where do you want to go and eat?'

'The benches at the back of the village green? I noticed it was in the sun as I came past. It should be nice.'

'Sounds perfect. Not worried about people seeing us out and about together?'

'That ship has sailed. Mum told me that Mrs Grigson called her the other day to say they'd not only seen us in the café together, but that apparently we'd been seen in Ripon together, too.'

Archer laughed in amazement. 'That woman does better research than a private eye. I wonder who spotted us in Ripon.'

'Who knows?'

'It's kind of sweet, though.'

She looked at him, surprised. 'You think so?'

'They may gossip, but isn't it good, too, to know that people are looking out for you?'

'You mean that they care?'

'Possibly. That they're keeping an eye out for you. I mean, if you were in danger, someone would step in. To have someone care about you, no matter their reason, is much better than having no one care, or no one noticing.'

'I guess I never thought about it like that.' He really was amazing, she thought. The way he considered things. But having learned more about his childhood, the way he and Axle were raised, she ought not to be surprised. His upbringing could have made him bitter, or angry. But he was neither of these things and his overt goodness, despite his past, made him very attractive indeed.

She drove them round to the green, parking up in a space by the village post office, and then they got out and found their bench, settling down and immediately being surrounded by hopeful birds. Sparrows. A random seagull that seemed huge enough to be an albatross. Starlings. A robin. 'I've been thinking about your offer.'

'Oh. Okay. What did you conclude?'

She sighed. 'I concluded that you may be right. I can't afford anything decent in this village. Prices have risen sharply since the pandemic and I'm not sure if you're aware but unemployed veterinary nurses don't have a steady wage.'

'Your mum's paying you, though, right?'

'Yes, but it's not much and it's not permanent. I need to be realistic.'

'Fair enough. So…?'

Haley sucked in a big gulp of air. 'So…it looks like I'll be taking you up on your offer to move in. I'll need to look at the place first, though. Make sure it's right for us all.'

'Wow. Okay.' He seemed happy and that warmed her heart. He wasn't doing this because it was simply practical, he really seemed to want her there.

It was scary. A huge decision and she still felt hesitant. She'd put herself out there once before and it had drastically backfired. If they took their time, did this slowly, then any kinks could be worked out before they became huge issues.

'But I won't move in just yet. Not until Mum is fully back on her feet.'

'Great.'

'But I do think we should establish some ground rules between us.'

'Agreed.'

'I contribute fairly with rent and bills.'

He nodded, listening, and took a bite of his sandwich.

'Before I move in, I get to prepare my room. I want to be able to move in and not have anything to do.'

'You mean decorate it?'

'If that's okay?' If he was going to get upset about something as simple as that, then maybe this wouldn't be a good idea.

But he simply nodded and smiled as he chewed.

'And I also guess we ought to decorate the nursery, too.'

'We'll do it together.'

'Okay. When can I come round to see it?'

'When are you free?'

'Hillary's coming over tonight with the twins to see their grandma. I could come round then?'

He gave a nod. 'Sounds good to me.'

'And one last rule.'

'What's that?'

'No flirting. No trying to make this more than it is. We don't need to make this complicated. We don't need to ruin something that could be really good,' she said, hoping on some level that he would be upset about that, or gasp and say, *Absolutely not!*

He smiled at her. 'I'll do my best.'

She forced a smile back at him. 'Good.' Feeling it wasn't that good at all.

He'd done what he could to smarten up the place before she came round. Not that he made much mess as a single guy. Archer considered himself to be quite good at keeping neat. He blamed it on the fact that when he was growing up, his mum didn't really pay attention to cleaning and so he needed to and he prided himself on picking up after him and Axle. It became a habit. Not to make mess. To wash dishes after cooking. To put dirty laundry in the wash. To hang it immediately out to dry, so that it didn't crease too much, because he hated ironing. And he'd learned over the years how to make a home. Houseplants were good.

Lots of greenery. Some decent art on the walls. Candles looked good. A throw over the sofa. He'd kept colours quite neutral. White, cream, taupe. His statement pieces added the colour.

The room that he hoped would be Halley's he'd been using as a bit of an office, but if she moved in, that was okay. He could move his desk and chair into his bedroom, put up some shelves for his files and books, and the nursery was just being used for random stuff that had no actual place in the cottage yet. He stored his bike in there, but he could buy a storage shed for it and put it in the garden. There were some old boxes with his childhood stuff contained within, but he could go through that, or put it in storage beneath his bed or in the back of his wardrobe.

He was willing to make room for Halley and the baby. Willing to make room for them so that they could feel at home. So that he could be there at all times for his child. Having Halley there too would be a wonderful bonus and she'd made it clear that there couldn't be any flirting, so that was good, they both knew where they stood.

No flirting…that was going to be hard. He'd slept with this woman. Knew how she felt. Knew where to touch her to make her gasp, to make her purr with pleasure, and he'd be thrilled to hear those noises again. To make her happy, to make her forget the world, if just for a little while, whilst she lay in his arms.

Could he do that?

When his doorbell rang at seven o clock on the dot, he knew it was her. He'd showered and changed after coming home from work and put on some jeans and a tee. His hair was still a little wet from the shower, but he figured he still looked presentable.

'Hey, welcome to your possible future abode!' he said, opening the door wide and inviting her in.

As she walked in, he stooped to kiss her cheek in greeting.

She blushed, which was cute. Watching her face develop rosy spots. 'Something smells nice.'

'Oh! Yeah, I'm baking some lemon twists for Barb.'

'Who's Barb?'

'One of the receptionists at work. It's her birthday tomorrow and she loves my lemon twists, so I make them for her every year. I'll let you try one when they're out of the oven.'

'Sounds great, thanks.'

'No problem. So, do you need a drink first, or do you want to get straight on down to business?' That sounded odd, so he cracked a grin, to show he was joking.

Halley smiled. 'Tea would be great, if you have any?'

He smiled back. 'I have plenty of tea. Decaf or normal?'

'Er, decaf, please.'

'Milk and sugar?'

'Milk, one sugar.'

'Coming right up.' He started to walk down the hallway and then stopped. 'Guess I can start some of the tour here. This is the hall, as you can see. Probably wide enough to get a buggy in, wouldn't you think?'

She nodded, looking about her. 'It's very light.'

'It's the mirrors. I saw it on a show once.' He paused in a doorway to his right. 'This is the lounge. Kitchen's at the end at the back of the house.' He watched her step into the lounge and take a look around. Saw her gaze land on his film poster, then drift on over to his bookshelves. A small smile lit her face as she went over and perused the titles on them.

'You weren't kidding about liking fantasy.'

'I never kid about my fantasies.' Oops. He was doing it again. But he was nervous! Couldn't help it. He wanted this to go right. 'Sorry, I meant...'

She laughed and waved it away as if it were nothing, then turned away to look at the rest of the room. 'Open fireplace.'

'Yep. But we could put a safety guard in front, you know, for when baby starts crawling and walking on its own. And this cottage is usually pretty warm, so I only tend to really use the fire when winter hits hard.'

'That must be nice? A real fire.'

'It can be. Would be nicer to share it with someone.'

Another smile.

'Want to see the kitchen?'

'Mmm-hmm.'

He led her back into the hallway and to the kitchen. When he'd first moved in, it had been much smaller, but he'd knocked a wall through into an old outhouse and really opened it up, with skylights and bifold doors that led out to the garden. Then he'd ripped out the old wood-effect kitchen and installed a new one that was glossy white with marbled surfaces.

'Wow. Looks amazing. No wonder you love to cook in here.'

He laughed. 'I dabble when I can.' He flicked the switch on the kettle and got out a couple of mugs and began to make tea. When he turned to glance at her to see what she might be thinking, he was surprised to see such a concerned look on her face. 'What's wrong?'

She paused before answering. 'Nothing.'

'No. There's something. What is it?' He went to her. Stood in front of her, trying to work out what was wrong and if he could help.

'It's just…this all seems so grown up, doesn't it? Moving in with someone? Sharing their living space. Do you think we might be rushing into something we might both regret?'

'Do I think we're making a mistake in coming together to raise this baby? No. I don't.'

'You don't have any doubts whatsoever?'

His only doubt was whether he'd be able to stop thinking about Halley in ways she'd plainly told him she didn't want. Halley had been the girl of his dreams for years as a child and now she was back in his life. More beautiful than ever and carrying his baby. He knew what it was like to be with her physically. To be with her in other ways? Mentally? Emotionally? Yeah, that was going to be an adjustment. 'Living with someone is always going to be weird, when you first do it. Our situation, though unique, is not strange. I think it's something that we have decided to do after thinking of all the alternatives, because the alternatives of raising this baby in separate homes isn't something either of us want. We want more for our child. We're on the same page, for our child, and that means something. We want...' he smiled '...we want our child to have everything that we didn't and we're both committed to making that happen. I've never shared my space with anyone before and I've always been protective of my home space. It's just for me. But now my world isn't just about me any more. It's about you and our baby. So I want to share it, because I feel safe here and I know that you could feel the same way. That our child could feel the same way. So no. I don't have any doubts about *that*. Do you?'

Were there tears in her eyes? Yes. There were.

'Not when you put it like that, no.'

He passed her her tea. 'Want to see your room?'

She took a sip, then nodded. 'I'd like that.'

Her bedroom-to-be was a good size. As big as his, it seemed, and yes, it had felt strange to peer into his bedroom and know that she had been intimate with this man and she was now standing over his bed.

She'd not known what to expect on entering his home. Would he have the typical bachelor pad? Would it be bare and sparse, the fridge empty of any real food and a gaming console sitting in front of the TV in a mass of cables and wires?

But there'd not been any of that. There'd been thought put into the decor. It looked comfy. There were throws and pillows on the couch. No gaming console to be seen, but there'd been lots of bookshelves and even a guitar, on a stand, that hung on the wall. He had art and lots of lots of green, trailing house-plants. It was clean, and properly clean, too. He'd clearly not quickly whizzed around the cottage with a hoover and duster, but done it properly, and there were diffusers in each room and lots of lights. The kitchen had been modern and minimalist, his only clutter on show a mass of fresh herbs growing on the windowsill and a spice rack filled with pots and flavours of all kinds. He'd told her he liked to cook and he clearly did. He was even baking right now for one of his staff at the surgery!

Upstairs, his room had the clean, mini-malist look, too. His bedspread was spotless, his pillows fluffy and he had this amazingly soft-looking bed runner and she'd itched to reach out with her hand to stroke it. But she'd stopped herself. What would it look like if she stroked his bed? Wouldn't that send the wrong message? Pregnant with his baby and looking as if she was longing to rip back the sheets and lie down?

Her room-to-be was tidy, but filled with random things. A desk. A chair. Lots of box folders stacked against a wall. But it had a good-sized window and plenty of floor space if it was emptied out. She'd easily fit a double bed in here. A wardrobe. A dressing table. A cot, if she had the baby in with her to begin with. Hillary had told her she might want to do that in the early days when she was still breastfeeding.

'It just makes it easier.'

'You could do whatever you wanted to make this home for yourself. Paint it. Wallpaper it. I could help you, if you want? I'm a pretty dab hand at all of that.'

'You're good at DIY, too?' she asked.

'When you grew up the way I did, you learned how to do a lot of things for yourself.'

'All right. Thanks. I might take you up on that offer.'

'Do. I'd rather you didn't start climbing ladders and balancing on them, whilst you're pregnant.'

He was being protective. She liked that. And to be honest? She'd never been good at painting or wallpapering. She'd tried it in her flat in Edinburgh and she'd made a good hash of it, wishing afterwards that she'd had the money to pay a proper painter and decorator.

'Let me show you where we could have the nursery.'

She followed him through to the next room, that was much smaller. Almost a box room. But it looked out over the rear aspect of the property, over the garden, and right next to the window, on the left-hand side, was a beautiful cherry tree. 'That must look lovely in spring.'

'It is, when it blossoms. Plenty of fruit on it right now. Actually, I just picked a lot of it, if you want to take some home to eat, or make a cherry pie?'

'Mum loves cherry pie.'

'I'll make sure I give you some, then. So what do you think? Big enough? It could fit a cot, a changing station, and I thought we could even fit in one of those rocking chairs with a footstool, to make any night feeds easy.'

'You've thought this through.'

'Haven't you?'

'Yes. I have.' But it was nice to know that he had, too. He was making a grand gesture and putting in a lot of effort. Opening up his home to her, sharing his space, so that they could do this together. Plus, living with him would protect her reputation in the village. Everyone would think them a couple and that was fine by her. No one would have to know the truth of their situation. Even if she did yearn for it to be different and exactly what the village thought it was.

'There's a big DIY store out at the industrial estate past Ripon. We could go there when you're next free and pick out paint, or wallpaper.'

She nodded, looking around at the room, imagining herself in here with a baby. 'Sure. I guess we ought to wait past the first trimester before we do anything. After we've seen the first scan and know everything's all right.'

'Have you got a date for that?'

'I'm still waiting to hear, but it should be soon, my doctor said.'

'Are you taking your folic acid?'

She smiled. 'I am.'

'That's great. Good.'

'And what colour were you thinking for in here? Do you have any ideas?'

'I guess it depends on whether we want to find out the sex. Or we stick to classic neutrals and not find out at all. Or we could go crazy and paint a fantastical mural on the walls, like in that shop?'

'I think I'd want to find out what we're having first. What about you?'

'I think I'd want that too.' He smiled at her for a long time and she was struck by the urge to go over to him and kiss him. To stand before him, lay her hand gently against his chest and then just kiss him.

But she fought the urge, pushing it away hard, because this was complicated enough without them making it into something else it wasn't ready for. That she wasn't ready for, even though every part of her was screaming at her to go to him. 'Then we're agreed?'

'We are.'

Okay, standing here in this small room, with him so close to me looking all sexy with his damp hair and his gorgeous brown eyes is simply too much!

'Sorry, I…er…need the bathroom. Just excuse me, would you?'

'Sure! I'll meet you back downstairs. I need to take those lemon twists out of the oven.'

'Great!' She fled to the bathroom, locking the door behind her and letting out a big sigh. Her feelings for Archer Forde were getting a little out of control. Maybe it was hormones or something? A deep-seated biological drive to stay with the father of your child for protection whilst the female was vulnerable? Feeling attracted to him to offer him sex and keep him interested? It had to do with something stupid, like her lizard brain, but she simply couldn't have it!

If she slipped up and kissed Archer Forde, it would put all of this at terrible risk and then where would she be?

The lemon twists were slightly more brown than he would have liked, but he'd forgotten all about them whilst showing Halley the house and the bedrooms and then, when they'd stood discussing the baby, about finding out the sex and she'd looked at him, all warm and smiley? Her beautiful blue eyes staring into his? He'd felt something pass between them that had scared the living daylights out of him!

I wanted to kiss her! Imagine how I would have ruined everything if I'd done that!

She'd just agreed to move in. She'd not agreed to him making a move on her. That sort of thing would have scared her off, for sure!

Thank God she went to the bathroom, so I could breathe again.

He heard her footsteps behind him as he was transferring the twists onto a cooling rack.

'Smells great.'

'Want to try one?'

'Maybe when they've cooled down.'

'Okay.' He turned and pressed himself back against the kitchen units to stay as far away from her as possible. Perhaps avoiding temptation from the get-go was the best thing and now that he was aware that his attraction for her was still there, it was best to take steps to avoid it.

'Archer, we do need to talk about what it will be like for us. Living together, I mean. What rules we need in place.'

'We've already agreed to no flirting.'

She smiled. 'Yeah. I don't want to ruin this situation by anything happening between us. You understand, don't you?' she asked with imploring eyes.

She really meant this—he could tell. She couldn't risk anything happening between them, either.

'I do. I very much do. We're both singing from the same hymn sheet, don't you worry,' he agreed. Of course he agreed. But he still wasn't prepared for the wave of sadness that washed over him as he realised that, by agreeing to that, he would never get to be with Halley the way he'd always wanted. It was like being surrounded by the ocean, with nothing to drink. She was there. She was with him. But she wasn't his.

And never could be.

Not if they wanted this living situation to work.

CHAPTER SEVEN

THE SMELL OF paint was making her feel nauseated, so Archer told her to go and put her feet up in the garden and he'd carry on with painting her bedroom-to-be. She'd fallen in love with a soft grey colour and had found a ridiculous fluffy lavender lamp that she'd decided to work her colour scheme around. It looked as if it had ostrich feathers on it, but she'd fallen in love with it and, after that, any other colour just hadn't seemed right.

Archer had covered the carpet with plastic sheets, moved out all the office stuff he'd had in there, as well as his bike, and emptied it completely for when she wanted to bring over furniture. But right now, he was using a roller to paint the walls. To start with, she'd assisted, offering to go around the edges of the windows and doors and to paint the corners where the walls met, but the aroma of paint had become too much for her still sensitive stomach to handle and so now she sat in the garden, on a sun lounger, beneath the morning sun, pretending to read one of the new fantasy books that Archer had bought her.

Instead, she was watching him through the window. He was wearing some old jeans and a tight white tee that he'd clearly used for decorating before as it was already covered in splashes and old fingerprint smears in white and taupe. From here, she could see the muscles in his arms as he pushed the roller up and then pulled it down again and she had to admit he was a fine figure of a man.

She felt herself stir and feel a yearning for him. Someone she couldn't have. Her hormones were driving her crazy. Sick she might be feeling, but her sex drive was still on full power! It was driving her crazy! From the open window, she heard him receive a phone call on his mobile.

'Oh, hi, Jenny. What's up?'

She watched him listen as he spoke to one of his partners at the practice. Halley liked Jenny and she could see why he and Jenny were friends. And now there was another old college friend that had appeared on the scene. James. James was another new vet at the practice, after Jenny had to go part time to help look after her mum with dementia.

'And what were the findings on the X-ray? Okay. Okay.' His voice dropped and he went solemn. 'Well, if they're able to wait I can pop in and have a chat with them. Sure. Okay. See you in ten.' He ended the call and looked out of the window to her. 'I've got to pop to the surgery. Will you be all right here on your own?'

'Problem?'

'A client who wants my opinion on a case. They know me, they're not used to Jenny.'

'I could tag along?'

He smiled. 'Okay. Five mins. I just need to change.'

'Okay.'

She swallowed hard as he walked away, pulling off his tee shirt. She got a too-brief glimpse of his muscular back and she groaned quietly. 'Seriously?' she muttered, getting to her feet and ambling back into the house.

She pottered about in the kitchen, rinsing the cups they'd used for tea earlier, and then Archer was there, in a new shirt and fresh jeans and smelling delicious, and she forced a smile. 'So, what's the case?'

'I'll fill you in on the way.'

It was a sad case, and one that Archer had been dealing with for a few years. The Taylor family had rescued a dog they'd found on holiday in Cyprus many years ago. They'd been at an outdoor restaurant and this mangy old hound had crept up to their table and begged for food. Tex, as they'd named him, had been skin and bone. His ribs visible, his face full of scars from fights and one or two scars on his body and hind quarters that Archer had identified as possible cigarette burns.

They'd discovered that Tex was probably still a young dog when they'd got him, about three years of age, and slowly, but surely, they'd brought him back to health. Tex was a great dog, and when his fur grew back they could see he was some kind of Labrador mix. But when Tex was five, Archer had diagnosed him with alimentary lymphoma. He'd become weak. Had developed sickness and diarrhoea on occasion. Was beginning to lose weight. The Taylors had decided they wanted to help Tex fight for his life as he was still a young dog and so they put him on chemotherapy.

Tex did well with the chemo. He didn't suffer too badly with any side effects and it had seemed as if his treatment was working. Only that morning, the Taylors had brought him back in, after noticing he was losing weight again and there was a lump on his chest, and when Jenny had taken an X-ray, she had discovered multiple tumours in his lungs and chest wall. The signs were not good and Jenny was recommending euthanasia, as signs were that Tex was in a great deal of discomfort and pain. The lymphoma had clearly come back and must have been metastasising quietly.

The Taylors wanted to talk to Archer. He'd kept Tex alive for them all these years and they wanted his opinion.

As he spoke to the owners, Halley offered to go out back and see Tex herself.

'I think the day has come where we need to make a careful decision,' Archer said to Jane and Kevin Taylor, knowing and hating the impact of his words. 'Tex has clearly had some advancement in his disease and we need to decide what is the best treatment for him going forward.'

Kevin looked quite pale. Jane was red-eyed from crying.

'He's only seven years old, Archer! It's too soon!'

He swallowed hard. He felt their pain. He'd hoped, too. He'd wanted this dog to beat the cancer. To reach a time they could say he was in remission and celebrate. But it had already been a long slog. Tex had fought for so long and now he was tired.

Archer had seen the same thing when he was with Amy. She'd fought as long as she could, but there just came a day when you had to say enough and accept the decision to stop. Animals were lucky. Their owners could pick a time for them and allow that time to be peaceful. Like going to sleep, without watching them suffer as the cancer or whatever disease it was ravaged their body. Amy had never had that choice, though he could remember her discussing going to that clinic in Switzerland.

'I know this is probably going to be one of the hardest things you'll ever have to do. But I've looked at the X-ray imaging myself and I have to say that I agree with my colleague.'

He waited for his words to sink in, struggling to maintain his own composure, but fighting for it. He liked Tex. He was a good dog. Good-natured. Friendly. A wonderful patient.

'But he's a fighter! Let's give him a chance to fight!' begged Jane.

He nodded. 'We have. He's been fighting for two years, but we have to look at the evidence. He has eight new tumours growing in his lungs and pleura. He has one tumour invading his abdomen, into his liver. He's losing weight and is clearly in great discomfort. I could continue to give him painkillers, but he would still be in discomfort and his quality of life would not be what you would wish for him.' He paused to let his words sink in. 'You have given him a good life. You saved him, more than once, and you love him dearly. But the best thing for him, the kindest thing for him, in my opinion, is to let him go now.'

His voice broke slightly and he had to clear his throat to regain control as Jane sank into her husband's arms and began to sob.

Kevin's eyes welled with tears. 'Can we spend some time with him before we...?'

Archer nodded. 'Of course. I'll bring him through.' He stepped out of the consulting room and into the back where they kept the animals that were inpatients. Halley was kneeling on the floor, scratching Tex's belly. He gave her a weak smile and knelt down beside her to give Tex a little scratch under his chin. As he knelt, Tex's tail thwacked against the floor in greeting.

'How's it going?' Halley asked.

'We're going to do the kindest thing,' he said, his voice soft, looking at this wonderful dog, who'd done nothing wrong and yet was having to have his life cut cruelly short. He felt his tears well up in his eyes and then Halley laid her hand upon his arm, then her head upon his shoulder.

'It's okay. It's for the best. You would never do this otherwise.'

He nodded, unable to meet her gaze, but grateful for her comforting touch. 'They want to spend a few moments with him. Could you bring him through?'

'Sure. But do you need a moment first? To say goodbye?' She looked up into his face and the care and concern she had for him was plainly there on her face and it all became too much.

The tears came then. He didn't often cry when he had to euthanise a pet, but there were some animals that just brought it out in him. Pets he'd known all their lives. Pets, like Tex, that had fought bravely against a cruel disease. Cases of animal cruelty where his tears came from a source of anger and frustration at what a human had done. Halley draped her arm around him and laid her head upon his shoulder again and he sank against her as he stroked Tex and rubbed his ears and told him what a good boy he was. The best. Then he sucked in a breath and stood up, squaring his shoulders, wiping at his eyes. Halley stood too and held his hand, passing him a tissue from a box on the side.

'Okay?'

'Yeah. I'm good.'

'You can do this.' She stroked his arm, her eyes full of compassion.

'I know. Okay, let's go.' He opened the door back into the consulting room and let Halley walk Tex through.

Tex stumbled a little, but his tail wagged furiously at seeing his mum and dad again and they sank to cuddle and kiss him.

'We'll be back in about ten minutes,' he said.

Halley took his hand and stepped out of the room with him.

Her heart ached for Archer. Seeing him so upset. So distraught. It was the hardest part of their job, having to do something like this. Halley hated having to be in the room when it was done, but she did it if the owners didn't feel strong enough to be there for the end. She would offer to go in and stroke the pet, so it wasn't alone. It was a privileged position to be in. To be able to confirm to the owners that their beloved fur baby had passed peacefully and without pain.

Tex had clearly meant a lot to Archer and now they were in the staff room at the back of the surgery, she made them both a strong cup of tea and sat him down on the couch. She sat next to him and held his hand.

It was meant to be a purely comforting thing. An *I'm with you* gesture. *You're not alone.* But as they sat there, she began to realise how much she didn't want it to stop. She liked holding his hand. Being this close to him. She liked that he wasn't pulling away from her. That he seemed to be drawing comfort from it and, weirdly, she realised how strong she felt, holding his hand.

Their teas sat on the low table, slowly going cold.

'It's times like this that make me second-guess having Jinx.'

His cat. His rescue cat. Jinx never seemed to be at the cottage when she called. She'd seen her once. Curled up on the sofa. 'Because you're worried about the day you'll lose her?'

He nodded. 'Their lives seem so fleeting sometimes and losing them hits us hard. They become such a strong part of our lives, our family. Why do we do it to ourselves?'

'Love. Companionship. Some people find it easier to be with animals than people.'

'I think it's that unconditional love. We can be whoever we want to be, act however we want to and a pet just won't judge us. They accept us. Love us back. No matter what. Who else in our lives gets that excited when we come home? Love that is unconditional is rare, don't you think? Humans don't love unconditionally. What a world it would be if we did.'

She nodded and squeezed his hand in hers. 'Animals don't get angry with us. They don't lie to us. They don't cheat. They don't abandon us at altars.' She smiled ruefully. 'They love to spend time with us. They think we're great. All the time. Even if we have just accidentally stepped on their paw, or told them off for doing their toilet in the house. They're innocent, aren't they? Not guilty of anything.'

'They just ask to be loved. That's all they want.'

'Isn't that what any of us want?'

He looked at her. Pondering her words, the tone she'd used. She'd sounded as though she was talking about herself. That she was saying she yearned for his love.

Halley blushed and reached for her cooling tea, taking a sip. It wasn't too bad. But she couldn't believe that that had slipped out. She wasn't asking him to love her. Even if sometimes she did dream of what real love, true love, felt like.

Archer let go of her hand as if electrocuted and stood up. 'I ought to go and do the deed. Not let it drag out. Have they had long enough alone, do you think?'

She glanced at the clock on the wall, grateful for the change in subject. 'It will never be enough time.'

'Would you come with me?'

She stared at him. Pleased that he wanted her there as his support. 'Of course. If you want me,' she added in a low voice.

'I do.'

Halley nodded and followed him through to the room where the Taylors and Tex waited.

Her mum was up and about in the kitchen, making herself a cup of tea. 'I've been thinking, love.'

'Oh, God, alert the media!' said Halley as she came through the front door, kicking off her work boots. She'd just spent two hours cleaning out the barn and she was exhausted.

Her mum gave her a look. 'I'm back on my feet now. I can do some things for myself and I don't want you out there lifting and carrying in your condition any more.'

'Well, you can't do it.'

'I know, so I've actually done more than just thinking. I've made a few phone calls.'

'To?'

'An employment agency. I've asked them to advertise for some farmhands and a temporary manager to take your place, until I'm fully fit again.'

'We've already got Paul and Will.'

'And they're great, but we need more help,

especially as we head towards autumn. Farms are great in the summer, but the colder months are much harder to get staff, you know that.'

'Okay.'

'You're happy with that?'

'It sounds sensible. I did think you were taking on too much and it will be a while until you're at full strength.'

'Good, and when the new staff start I want you to move in with Archer. Get settled into your new home and look after my precious grandchild.'

'There's plenty of time for that. Besides, we're still decorating.'

'And it will be done by the time I've got the new staff up and running. So, you can go.'

'You sound like you're trying to get rid of me.'

'Oh, love. I could never do that. But for a long time now I've been worried about you. Alone and up in Edinburgh. But now you're back and you're staying. And I have a chance to see my new grandchild whenever I want. But more than that…you have a chance to be happy and settled and not alone. With Archer.'

'It's not like that between us,' she said, knowing that it felt everything but.

'Isn't it? You made a baby.'

'We weren't trying to.'

'Maybe so, but you have and you're planning on raising that baby together and I so want you to be happy. After Piotr, I thought you'd never be happy again.'

'We're just friends,' she said, knowing that, in her heart, she felt so much more for him.

'And from friendships great loves are often born. How many couples do you hear say that they were friends first?'

'Archer's not looking for a romantic relationship, Mum.'

'Are you?'

It was hard to stand there under her mum's questioning stare, because the truth was that she craved to be loved. Craved to be adored and made to feel as though she was the only woman that any man could love. To be treated like a precious jewel. To be thought of when she wasn't there. To be missed, desperately. To be someone's whole world. She thought that maybe Archer might love a woman that way. 'I'm scared.'

'You can't live your life in fear, love. That's no way to live.'

'But what if I make a mistake?'

'We're human. We make mistakes. No one in this village, this world, is perfect. What matters is how we deal with the cards we're dealt. I understand why you retreated after

Piotr's wife appeared, but all these years you've been alone and I've felt so sad for you. You weren't living, love, you were existing! And now you have a rare chance. Archer's a good man and he loves deeply. You weren't here when he lost Amy, but I saw it in him. The way he took care of that girl when she was sick… He's been grieving a long time. Same as you. But together? I think you two could be something amazing. You just need to be brave enough to see it.'

Halley hugged her mum. She could see it. That was what scared her. She really appreciated everything her mum was saying. It meant a lot. But words were sometimes easy to say. Actions could sometimes be harder.

What if she took that chance and opened up her heart to Archer and he rejected it? What if he was still hurting and wasn't ready for the onslaught of her feelings? She knew she could be pretty full on sometimes and some guys might think it a bit much. Because when Halley fell in love, she went in all guns firing.

She wanted things to be good between her and Archer. That way, her baby would have its father around all the time. But if she scared him off before this baby got here…? Then losing him would be all her own fault. And she wasn't sure she wanted to carry that guilt. Archer had said nothing to her about his feelings for her. But he had said plenty of what he wanted for their baby. So she wasn't sure what he felt and she wasn't ready to take a chance on exposing her vulnerable heart to someone she still wasn't sure of.

It just seemed a terribly deadly mistake to make.

CHAPTER EIGHT

TWO LOVELY YOUNG girls responded to the employment agency advert and had begun working at the farm and a new part-time manager was learning the ropes, earning Halley a lie-in most mornings, for which she was eternally grateful. Now, in the mornings, she could take her time getting up. There was no need to get up at four a.m., don overalls and wellies and go out to feed the animals and muck them out, ready for the public's adoring eyes at nine.

The last few days, she'd not even bothered with an alarm clock. She'd got up when she felt like it. Stretched, donned a dressing gown and headed downstairs to get breakfast.

Her mum, an eternal lark, would already be up, and now she was able to get around much more easily and climb the stairs, as long as she took it slowly. On this morning, Halley could hear her downstairs in the kitchen, doing God only knew what, and was that the radio she could hear? It sounded like voices. Was Mum talking to someone? It was probably the new manager, Clark. He kept popping in to double-check things, so it was probably him.

Halley headed downstairs, yawning and sleepy, and stepped into the kitchen to find her mum and Archer there, sitting at the table.

'Archer! What are you doing here?'

He smiled and stood up to greet her. 'Your mum invited me over for breakfast.'

'Oh! She didn't tell me she was doing that.' She gave her mum a look that said *I know what you're up to*.

Her mum laughed. 'It's nothing like that. I'm not scheming. I just thought it might be nice for Archer to join us before work and tell you the news.'

'What news?'

'Our veterinary nurse, Anu, is leaving. She's met a guy who lives in Hull and she's upping sticks and going to live with him. She put her notice in yesterday and I thought that you might be interested in taking on the post until your maternity leave begins.'

Halley stared at him. 'You're joking?'

'No joke.' He smiled and held out her chair for her to sit down.

She sank into it, then turned to face him.

'You're serious? You want us to not only live together, but also work together?'

'It's only part time, so not a heavy workload, and this way you'd have a job waiting for you, after the baby, if you wanted it.'

'I think it'll be perfect, love. I know how independent you like to be,' said her mum. 'It would get you out of the house and earning money and, like Archer says, you'll have a real job waiting for you, if you decide you want to work afterwards. And it's only part time, so you wouldn't be away from the baby for too long.'

'Sounds like you two have got it all worked out.'

Archer shook his head. 'There's no pressure to take it. None whatsoever. I just thought I'd give you first refusal, that's all. I'm still going to advertise in *The Gazette*, if need be. So take your time and think about it.'

She nodded. 'Okay.'

'And I have news, too,' said her mum.

'Oh?'

'I'm properly back on my feet now. I'm able to look after myself. I can shower alone. I can work a little bit. I don't need you and Hillary babysitting me any more.'

Halley felt a wave of heat wash over her. 'You're evicting me?'

'No, love! You can stay here for as long as you want! But I am saying, I don't need you to stay. If you want to stay here and have the baby here, then that's fine by me. But if you wanted to move in with Archer, then I'm okay now.'

Halley glanced at Archer.

He was smiling at her, the hope in his eyes almost too much to take.

She'd known this day was coming. But it had always been this hypothetical day, far into the future, and it was easy to agree to hypotheticals, but to actually *act* on them? To move in with Archer? When she had all these feelings for him? What if she screwed everything up? Her mum was giving her the option to take a safer route. Stay here at the farm and have the baby. But if she chose to, she could take a risk and move in with Archer.

'It's a lot to take in suddenly,' said Archer, as if noticing her hesitation. 'We've spoken about it, but actually doing it is scary, right?'

She nodded, glad that he understood.

'There's no pressure from me, Halley. My home is yours and there for you, whenever you need.'

But she knew how much he wanted her there, so he could be there for his baby. And the first scan was coming up soon and she'd already imagined it in her head. Both of them leaving the house together to go to the hospital.

But from which house?

The farm?

Or Archer's?

Theirs.

Sanjay had brought Jess back in for a follow-up check on her abscess and Archer was pleased to see that the abscess was virtually undetectable and the bite wound from their resident cat, Badger, had healed and scabbed over nicely. Jess's temperature was back to normal and Sanjay reported that everything was going much better.

'We took it back a few steps with introducing them. Swapped their litter trays over so they could get used to each other's scents. Swapped toys and someone suggested giving them each other's blankets covered in a little catnip to play with before introducing them again to mellow them out a bit and it seemed to work.'

Archer laughed. 'That'll do it. And how are they now?'

'They were a little hesitant after the catnip had worn off, but they swiftly realised they wanted to be friends and last night they even washed each other a little bit.'

'That's great!'

Sanjay nodded. 'I'm so happy, I really am. I didn't want this to fail, you know? A lot was riding on this successful introduction.'

'Well, it takes animals *and* people some time to get used to living with someone new.'

'Oh, yeah! I heard Halley Campbell has moved in with you. You two are a couple. Having a baby. Congratulations!'

'Thanks.' He didn't correct Sanjay. He didn't tell him that they weren't a couple. Not really. It was just easier to let everyone assume that they were and, so far, the feedback had been positive.

'How's that going?'

'Well, it's only been two days, but, yeah, it's going great!'

'Good for you, man. I'm glad you've found some happiness.'

'Thanks. I'm glad that Jess has, too.' He pulled open the door to end the consultation and when Sanjay was gone, he closed it again and let out a breath. So the grapevine had caught up, then, and the whole village probably knew by now. He and Halley would be the high topic for a little while, but it would die down. And at least this time they were being talked about for a good reason. Yes, gossip could be a bad thing, but this was good. People were *happy* for them. That showed they cared.

Halley moving in had been both exciting and terrifying and they were both still in that stage where they were gently tiptoeing around the other person, trying not to get in each other's way, or space. But it was so hard when all he wanted to do was just sit next to her on the couch and eat popcorn whilst watching a movie together. He'd suggested it last night, but she'd got this frightened look in her eye and said she was tired and gone to bed early. That told him plenty. That even though she'd moved in with him so he could be close to his child, she was not in a relationship with him and nor did she want to be.

Which is great. Because I'm not looking for one either.

He didn't need to. He had everything—almost everything—he'd ever wanted.

But he still felt it would have been lovely to snuggle on the couch. Maybe under a blanket? As friends, if nothing more?

Would they ever get to that stage, where they felt comfortable with one another?

Or maybe I should sprinkle us both in catnip...?

* * *

'Are you ready?'

Halley nodded. 'As I'll ever be. Are you?' It was the morning of their first scan appointment at the hospital to check on their baby. Halley was thirteen weeks exactly and starting to feel the effects of the morning sickness ebbing away. Each day was getting better and she was actually starting to feel good now, instead of constantly battling endless nausea that got worse each evening.

'I'm nervous. I'm just hoping everything's all right.'

'I think everyone feels that way. I just wish I could go to the loo. My bladder is so full, but they need it for the scan imaging to be clearer. I just hope I don't pee myself when they push down on it.'

'I'm sure lots of mothers feel that way.'

'I guess they do.'

Archer opened the front door and stepped out, turning back to close the door behind her so he could lock it, but he stopped and stared at her, frowning. 'You okay?'

'What if there's something wrong? What if…they find something? Or worse, find nothing at all and there was never a baby, and I'm one of those women that has a hysterical pregnancy or—?'

'Hey.' Archer stepped back in and took hold of her upper arms. 'It's all going to be fine. We have to believe that and let's keep on believing that unless they tell us otherwise. Okay?'

She looked up at him, tearful and afraid. 'I don't know why I'm feeling like this.'

'I do.' He smiled. 'You're being a mother. A protective mother. You want your child to be healthy. You want your child to pass this first test. You've got used to the idea of being a mother and the idea that someone could take that away? That's terrifying.'

He was right. She had got used to the idea. And she'd changed her entire life around it! She'd left Edinburgh, she'd moved in with a man that she was trying her very hardest not to love, but it was difficult because he was so damned lovely all the time! Understanding and kind and thoughtful. He was perfect. And so if there was no baby…her entire life would come crashing down around her ears and she couldn't go through something like that again.

'Are you terrified, Archer? Are you scared to death that someone could take away your being a father?' She needed to know. It was important. She needed to know that she wasn't the only one stranded on a tiny raft in the middle of the ocean, here. She needed to know he was with her. That he felt the same way on this, at least. It was like standing in that church again, staring at Piotr's wife, knowing that at any moment her happiness was about to be snatched away. That it had all been pretend and never real.

But the way he was staring deeply into her eyes…the way that he was standing so close… Could she reach out? Could she pull him in tight and not let go? The urge to have him hold her, to stroke her hair, to whisper soothing words in her ear, was just so powerful!

'I am. I'm scared of it all,' he said in a low voice, his gaze going from her eyes to her lips and then back again.

And she felt it. Like a punch to the gut. That he was feeling some kind of way about her, too. This wasn't just about the baby! Maybe, just maybe, Archer had had some feelings about her, too.

And that scared her even more.

She broke the intense eye contact and took a step back, smiling awkwardly. 'We ought to get going. We don't want to be late and fail *our* first test at being parents.'

Though she felt sure the actual first test had been when the test turned positive and she'd had to tell him about the baby.

He'd passed that first test with flying colours and had continued to pass the fatherhood test ever since. She would not fail her baby by screwing that up.

She would not, *could* not, kiss Archer Forde—no matter how much she wanted to.

The waiting room was bright and cheery. White walls, with modern art in splashes of red, blue and yellow, beneath skylights that streamed in sunshine. On one wall was a vending machine filled with chocolate and crisps. Next to it, a water dispenser, with those weird polystyrene cups with pointed bottoms, so you couldn't actually put them down, but had to sit there holding them, until you were done.

It was very busy. Almost full. Filled with women of all shapes and sizes. Women like herself in the early stages, with no discernible bump yet. Those that were a bit further on, maybe midway, and those that looked ready to burst. In a far corner was a children's play area and in it a couple of toddlers played.

She and Archer found seats over by the doors to the toilets and breastfeeding room. Her nerves were running amok and her teeth even began to chatter, so Archer reached out and took her hand and held it. 'Deep breaths.'

Halley laughed nervously. 'I'm trying. But this room is making everything all so real! We're actually here because we're having a baby. A baby! And we're about to see it. The thing that's been making me ill the last couple of months.'

'The thing?' Archer smiled, raising an eyebrow.

'Don't!' She laughed. 'I'm nervous enough as it is.'

'I know. We'll be fine. You'll see.'

She loved that he had this steadfast belief that everything would be all right. He was a calm port in a storm. A rock. Where did that come from? Was it because he had to be the grown-up for his little brother when they were young? He'd told her about his mother and how she used to be. How she'd made him feel, as a child. Had he always been this sensible and level-headed?

Halley looked at the other couples. Some looked bored. Others nervous, like her. One or two looked worried. Did they have problems? If they had problems, then did that mean that she wouldn't?

Don't be ridiculous. That's not how it works.

But she wanted it to work that way. And she knew she was only hoping for that because she was scared, even if it did make her feel bad for wishing bad stuff onto other people.

I'm human. I'm not logical. Especially when it comes to protecting my own.

Maybe Archer was right and this was her motherly instinct kicking in? For such a long time after Piotr, she'd believed that she'd never get to be a mother. She'd shut down that part of her that hoped and wished for the white picket fence and the perfect husband and the two adorable children. One boy. One girl. Maybe a dog. Some chickens in the backyard. She'd told herself she'd never have it, because she didn't think she could trust any man to get close enough to get married and have kids. And yet here she was. Archer might not be in love with her and they weren't married, but they were living together and, whilst there was no white picket fence, there was a cute cottage and a privet hedge. There was room for a dog and some chickens, if they wanted.

Her full bladder ached. And she desperately wanted to go to the loo. But more than that, she so wanted to be in that room and finally have one of her life's dreams come true. To see her baby on the screen. To be told that everything was going perfectly. To hear its heartbeat. Would that happen today? Or was it too early? She'd seen women on TV or in films have it done and a few people she followed online, when they'd shared a video of having it done, and it always seemed such a magical moment.

Halley so wanted a magical moment! Happiness, just lately, had seemed like something she'd always had to chase and it was always just out of reach, almost as if the universe were teasing her. She watched as women went into the rooms and came out again about twenty minutes or half an hour later. So far, they'd all come out with smiles on their faces, clutching scan pics. Would she be one of them, too?

'Miss Halley Campbell?'

'Yes.' She stood and Archer stood with her, letting go of her hand—he'd been holding it all this time—so that she could walk ahead of him into the room.

The room was darkened. The ultrasound machine was to the left, with the two wand devices on it. One long and thin, the other looked a little like a hammerhead. Above it, the screen. Next to that, the examination couch and beside that, a chair.

'Hello, Halley, my name is Sunita and I'm going to be scanning you today. Can you confirm your date of birth for me?'

Halley told her.

'And your full address and postcode?'

Once she'd given the information, Sunita asked her to pop onto the bed. 'If you could lift your top a little and lower your trousers down a little? I'm just going to tuck this paper into the top of your underwear to protect it from the gel. It'll feel a little cold to start.'

Halley nodded and nervously got onto the bed.

'When was the date of your last period?'

Halley confirmed the date and undid her trousers and lay back nervously.

Archer sat on the chair beside the bed and held her closest hand.

She squeezed it back as the sonographer squirted very cold gel onto her belly and then turned the screen towards her. 'I'll turn this back once I confirm everything first and then I'll show you, okay?'

'Okay.'

Halley knew they did this, but still she felt scared. What if she looked and there wasn't a baby? What if there was something wrong? What would she and Archer do then? They'd talked about many things, but they'd never once talked about what they'd do if there was something wrong with the baby. Archer had always said they shouldn't worry until they got told to worry. Was that the right approach?

It seemed an age before Sunita smiled and turned the screen. 'Here you go. There's your baby.'

Halley crooked her head back to look and then her heart just melted.

There it was! A little grey blob, with something fluttering in its chest.

My baby's heart.

'Oh, my God!' whispered Archer in awe.

'Everything looks good here. I'm going to take some measurements to confirm, okay?'

Halley nodded, physically unable to speak. All she could do was stare at the screen as Sunita zoomed in on various things. Measuring from crown to rump. Thigh length.

'Now I'm going to measure the nuchal translucency, okay? This is what tells us the risk for Down's Syndrome.'

'Okay,' said Archer, squeezing Halley's fingers tightly.

And she realised, in that moment, that it didn't matter. It didn't matter if they found anything wrong, because she would love this baby, no matter what. The sickness she'd experienced was forgotten and forgiven. The cravings that had made her lose precious sleep and get up in the middle of the night knowing she needed chocolate ice cream and pickles was fine. The headaches. The bloating. The exhaustion.

None of it mattered.

All that mattered was the baby. Her baby. *Their* baby.

'Measurements are good. Nuchal translucency is in a healthy range. Want to hear the baby's heartbeat?'

Halley nodded.

Sunita pressed a button and suddenly there it was, filling the room with a steady, rhythmic sound.

'That's amazing!' said Archer.

She felt tears sting her eyes. Happy tears. How was this happening? How were all her dreams coming true? She felt as though she could lie on that bed all day and listen to that sound.

'That's it. All done. I've printed you off some pictures.' Sunita handed her a long roll of ultrasound pics as she helped wipe some of the gel off her belly.

'Thank you,' Halley managed, sitting up, then standing, to do up her trousers and gaze at the pictures.

'We'll contact you soon with the date of your next scan, okay? We usually do it around the twenty-one-weeks mark.'

'Thank you.'

The waiting room was so bright it hurt their eyes. But they left the room smiling and gazing at the pictures, pointing out features as they made it out to the car. When she got into the front passenger seat, Halley began to cry.

'Hey! What's wrong?' His arm went around her shoulders.

She looked at him, knowing she was ugly crying, but not caring, because silly little things like that didn't matter any more. 'Nothing! Nothing's wrong, I'm just...'

He pulled her as close as he could, pressed his lips to the top of her head.

'I know. You're happy.' He kissed her again. 'So am I.'

She turned to look at him. 'How did we get so lucky, Archer?'

He stared back at her. 'I don't know. But I'm glad that we are.'

Archer drove them home, feeling a lot less tense than when they'd set out that morning. The first scan had been playing on his mind a lot and so whenever Halley had started worrying about it too, he'd wanted to take that worry away from her. It was wrong that she should carry it in her heart. She had enough to do with carrying the baby. He wanted to take the burden of everything else away from her.

But then to see his baby on that screen? And look down and see Halley's face, lit by tears of happiness? The world had suddenly felt right—until they'd got back into the car and he'd been comforting her and she'd turned to him, crying.

'How did we get so lucky, Archer?' she'd asked.

He'd not known the answer, but even if he had, he wouldn't have been able to say it, because all he could think of in that moment as she'd turned to him, gazing up into his eyes, all he could think of was how much he wanted to kiss her.

It was getting ridiculous now, these feelings that he kept having for Halley. He'd tried his best. He'd tried to force them away, to tell himself that they weren't ever anything he could act upon and so he should stop feeling that way. But they kept coming back. Day after day. And they'd got stronger ever since she'd moved in.

His head kept saying, *Yeah, but wouldn't it be great if you did? Remember that night on Rookery Point? How amazing it was? You could have that again.*

And yes, maybe he could and maybe it would be amazing, but what if it went wrong? What if he lost not only Halley but their baby, too? She could move out. Take the baby with her and then he'd be back to seeing his baby part time and gazing at Halley and wondering how it had all gone wrong.

But if he didn't kiss her, then he wouldn't be risking that, would he? He'd get to keep them both, because there was no reason why this couldn't work out. What they had right now.

And so he didn't kiss her. He painfully let go of her and started the engine. Drove them home, knowing that he was in this much deeper than he had ever realised and he would do anything to keep them both safe. And if keeping them safe meant ignoring how he felt, then he'd do it.

Because he couldn't risk losing either one.

CHAPTER NINE

ARCHER HAD OFFERED to take her out to dinner, now that she was feeling better and the first scan had confirmed that everything was fine. They had a little breathing room, a little time before their next scan and he wanted to celebrate that. The local veterinary association was having a fundraising night and so he'd told her to put on her best dress, because he was taking her for dinner and dancing.

It had been a long time since she'd been able to get all dressed up and have a fancy night and now that she was feeling better, she was looking forward to it.

But she'd not brought any fancy clothes back with her from Edinburgh, figuring all she'd be doing was working on a farm, and so she'd gone out to town and bought herself a dress and some heels.

Halley wasn't used to heels. She often felt like a newborn giraffe in them and feared for her ankles if something went wrong and so she'd spent that day practising walking in them.

'I told you—you look fine.' her mum said from the kitchen table where she was sipping a cup of tea. She'd taken her mum with her to get the outfit. A bit of a girls' day out. And her mum had wanted to stay to see the full effect before she headed back to the farm. Archer was upstairs, on the phone to Axle.

'It doesn't feel fine. I'm trying to look like a woman who knows what she's doing.'

'I think that ship has sailed, love.'

Halley laughed. 'I think maybe it has. What do you think? Will I pass?'

'Let's see. Walk over there.'

Halley strode purposefully from the kitchen and down the hall, pretending she was some model on a catwalk.

'Gorgeous, love.'

'You're not just saying that?'

'No!'

'Liar.'

Her mum laughed at Halley's rueful smile. 'I'm sure Archer will think you look amazing.'

'This isn't for him. It's for me.'

'Really?'

'Yeah.'

'All right.'

'Well, what does that mean?'

'It means I know you better than you do and I know that you like him a lot. If you think you're dressing up in that dress, with those heels, just for you, then you're more delusional than I thought.'

She made a shushing motion at her mum, afraid that Archer might overhear. 'Nothing's going to happen between Archer and me,' she whispered.

Her mum laughed. 'Your womb says something different, love.'

Halley frowned and stood in front of the mirror to check her reflection. Archer would come downstairs any minute to take her out for the evening. Okay, so maybe she had picked out a dress that would look amazing on her figure and she had thought about how it accentuated her hips and breasts, but she'd just wanted to feel attractive again. She'd been in overalls and wellies for a long time and hadn't had a proper night out for ages! And as the pregnancy progressed and she got bigger and more uncomfortable, she might not have another opportunity for a night out like this for an eternity!

I am doing this for me. But if Archer likes it too? Then that might just be a bonus.

* * *

When Archer came downstairs, he was blown away by the sight of Halley waiting for him in the living room. He was very much aware that her mum was sitting there, too, watching them both, and so he tried to carefully control his facial reaction. 'Wow! You look amazing.'

'She scrubs up well, doesn't she?' said Sylvie.

'She does.' He smiled, trying to calm the rush of his heart.

'Well, you look very nice too,' Halley said, her cheeks reddening from his praise.

Her dress was amazing, clinging to her in all the right places. Red silk that looked amazing against her long blonde hair. And then, as she took a step to the table to reach for a small clutch bag, he happened to notice the side split that revealed her leg up to her mid-thigh. He must have swallowed hard, or gulped, or something, because Sylvie was laughing.

'Right, my taxi's here. I'm off. You kids have fun and…er…don't do anything I wouldn't do.' Sylvie dropped a kiss on her daughter's cheek, gave Archer a quick hug and then she was gone, the front door closing behind her with some finality.

And he was alone with Halley. All of a sudden he felt as though he didn't want to go to this fundraiser at all. He didn't want dinner and he didn't want dancing. He wanted Halley. He wanted to take her by the hand, lead her upstairs, lay her on his bed and then go exploring beneath that dress!

He gave a nervous laugh.

'What's funny?' She was looking at him curiously.

'Nothing. Nothing's funny. You're beautiful, Halley, and seeing you in that dress caused some thoughts and for my blood supply to zoom in a direction away from my brain, so I stopped thinking properly for a moment there.'

She blushed.

He held out his arm. 'Are you ready, my lady?'

Halley smiled and stepped towards him. 'I am.' And she took his arm and together they headed outside to the car.

It felt good to know she'd affected him *in that way*. If you'd asked her weeks ago if she'd wanted to provoke that reaction in him she would have fervently said no, but in the last few weeks, she had changed. On a fundamental level.

Her whole life had changed, of course, and so had she. She was pregnant now. She was going to be a mother. She had moved in with

Archer, the father of that child, and she had become more and more aware of her feelings for him. She'd not believed he felt in any way about her, so for him to react so strongly to seeing her in the dress made her feel incredibly good!

I've still got it.

She was getting used to her new body. It felt different and though she knew that the changes, physically, were probably infinitesimal at this point, she still felt different. She felt bigger. Her boobs felt rounder. Her stomach bigger. She'd noticed her jeans were getting uncomfortably tight around the waist and, at the end of the day, she couldn't wait to take everything off and put on pyjamas. Elasticated waists had become her friend. Halley went to the loo more often and her bladder felt like the size of a pea. She ached in places she hadn't known it was possible to ache. Her stomach occasionally blew a gasket and either threatened eruption or demanded strange concoctions. She'd even started eating mushrooms and Halley hated mushrooms! Her skin kept breaking out in spots. Her hair always seemed to need a wash every day, instead of every couple of days. She was changing and she felt every part of it, no matter how small, so to still look good enough to cause a sexual arousal in Archer?

She'd take it. Of course she would. It was a powerful feeling and, having felt as if she'd lost her power when the blood test had confirmed she was pregnant and that her life was ricocheting down a road she hadn't chosen, she was glad to feel as if she might be back in control, after all.

The fundraiser was taking place in an old Edwardian building that had once been the home of a duke.

They arrived to find a queue of cars, waiting to park up, and when they finally found a place it was quite the walk to get inside.

The evening had become cool, and when she shivered, Archer felt it.

'You're cold.' He shrugged off his dinner jacket and stopped to drape it around her shoulders. It was lovely and warm and smelt of him. 'Better?'

She smiled up at him. 'Better. Thank you.'

His smile was everything and Halley was beginning to believe that maybe there was something there between them. More than just the baby. More than just his duty as a father. He liked her. She was sure of it. She could feel it in the look of his eyes. The way he held her hand. The way he stood beside her, almost protectively, as they queued on the stone steps to get inside. His hand in the small of her back. It was just a small touch. Nothing major. But she felt it with everything she had.

As they entered the hall a waitress stood there with flutes of champagne. He walked past her to get to the waitress who held flutes of orange juice, taking two and handing one to Halley.

'You can still drink, you know.'

'I'm driving.'

'You're allowed one, at least.'

'It's fine. I'll have what you can have.'

He was there for her, that much was clear. And every small thing he did? She noticed it. She *noticed*. She couldn't have alcohol, so neither would he. It was a simple thing for someone to do, but it meant something. It meant something coming from him.

Above them, great crystal chandeliers twinkled down upon the assembled guests below, who mingled in their couples and their groups, and then, somewhere off to the left, music started. Someone playing the piano. Halley didn't recognise the music, but knew it was something classical. Something famous. She just didn't know what it was called.

'Want to dance?' he whispered in her ear.

'I do,' she said with a smile.

They put down their drinks on a nearby table and Archer took her hand and led her out onto the dance floor, pulling her close when they reached the middle. He held one hand with his and the other was in the small of her back again and, gently, they began to sway.

Halley glanced at the other couples dancing. She didn't know anyone here and nor did she feel the need to. It was perfectly perfect knowing just Archer. She gazed up into his eyes and smiled at him. 'You're a good dancer.'

'It's just moving from side to side. I think anyone could manage this.'

'And you can't take a compliment.'

He smiled. 'Never had many.'

'Well, then, that's going to change. You are a good dancer and, yes, it may only be swaying from side to side, but you haven't stamped on my toes, so that makes you a good dancer in my eyes.'

'Why, thank you.'

'And…it feels good to be dancing with you.'

Did she feel him stiffen then?

'Thanks.'

'I mean it, Archer. I'm enjoying being here with you tonight.'

'Me, too. But then I'm with the most beautiful woman in the room, so it's not a hardship.'

Her other hand rested on his upper arm. She could feel him tense beneath his suit, felt his chest against hers inhale a large, steadying breath. She wished she could place her spare hand on it, to feel how fast his heart was going. If it was going as fast as hers, that would tell her something.

She looked up to his face, hoping he would meet her gaze, but he was looking at anyone but her. 'Hey. I'm down here.'

He glanced at her then, as if to say, *What? I know. I know you're there.* But then he looked away again.

And she got frightened then, because what if she'd been imagining all of this? All this attraction that she hoped he felt? Maybe he was just the kind of guy that was empathetic? Maybe he was just the kind of guy that was polite? Maybe he was just the kind of guy that knew how to treat a woman right, but was still unable to allow one close?

They'd started this whole relationship off by making it clear to one another, on top of Rookery Point, that they weren't looking for a relationship. That neither of them needed or wanted that.

Ever!

Was she trying to push him in a direction he wasn't ready for? She did this. Rushed into things. Let her emotions run away with her, and could she trust them right now, fuelled as they were with hormones?

'I'm sorry, Archer.'

Now he looked at her, frowning. 'For what?'

'I don't know. I—' She couldn't speak any more. The words got stuck in her throat.

What could she say? *I'm sorry for trying to push this in a direction you're not ready for it to go. I'm sorry for thinking that you might be attracted to me and want more.*

As her throat closed, she felt a panicked feeling and knew that she had to get out. Had to get some air.

'Excuse me.'

She pulled herself free of his embrace and made a dash through a small break in the crowd, leaving him behind. The further she got from him, the more she felt she could breathe, but the more the tears stung the backs of her eyes. She didn't know where to go. Which way was out. So she pushed against the crowd that was still coming in through the front doors and ran down the steps and out towards the gardens, stopping only when she came across a willow tree. She parted the fronds to pass through and hid underneath, leaning against the tree trunk and wiping her eyes.

Had she just made an utter fool of herself?

Archer would be full of questions when he found her. And what would she say? Tell him the truth? That she was having these deep feelings for him and wanted to take their relationship further? But that she was afraid he would say no? But that she was even more afraid he'd say yes? Maybe he'd even go so far as to say it was just her hormones, or something! Caused by the pregnancy and that she'd feel different later.

No. I don't think he would say that. That's me. Worrying that it might be true.

Because for all these years she'd kept herself single. Had dated, yes, but never let it get serious. Had scratched an itch when she'd felt the need. But she'd never felt tempted enough by a man to cast aside all her protective walls and expose her vulnerable heart and soul and be brave enough to take a chance with someone else.

Until Archer.

So maybe the pregnancy, the baby, *was* the defining variable here?

It was the only thing that was different!

Or was it?

When else had she met a man like Archer? He wasn't superficial. He didn't care more about himself than he did anyone else. He was kind, empathetic, a good listener, intelligent, funny. He was a great vet! Unselfish, support-ive, steadfast in his beliefs about what would make a good father.

But had he ever expressed how he felt about being a good partner? A good boyfriend or even a good husband?

No. He spoke about the baby and only the baby. He was with her and had her in his life because of that one variable. No other reason.

I need to get a grip here. We had a good scan. The baby is healthy. We heard its heart. I'm feeling better and I'm here at this beauti-ful place to have a good time! So I need to let myself do that!

Sheepishly, she dabbed at her eyes, sucked in a deep breath and pushed herself away from the tree and headed back towards the house.

It did look beautiful, all lit up at night. She was in a beautiful dress and she felt good in it and they were meant to be celebrating. Hal-ley knew she needed to allow herself to do that. As she climbed the steps, she saw Archer standing at the top.

'There you are! I've been looking all over—are you all right?'

She laughed. Smiled. Nodded. 'I just needed some fresh air all of a sudden, that's all.'

'You're sure?'

'Absolutely.'

As she got closer he touched her arm.

'You're cold!'

'I'm okay! Honestly, let's go inside.'

'Okay. If you're sure you're okay… I think everyone's about to head through to the dining room to eat now.'

'Great! I'm starving.'

He seemed a little perplexed, but she felt that she'd managed to explain herself. Archer would never know the truth of what she'd been feeling and maybe that was a good thing. Maybe she could keep her feelings to herself until *after* the baby was born and re-evaluate then.

'You're sure you're feeling all right? Because if you're not, we can go home. We don't have to stay.'

'Hey! I was promised a night of dining and dancing and I want that. When else will I get the chance again at a place such as this?'

He nodded, but she could see he was holding back some scepticism, so she was determined to prove to him that she was having a good time.

They were sat at a table of eight and spent some time introducing themselves to the other guests. Halley had Archer on her left, but on her right was a young woman who'd recently been voted Veterinary Surgeon of the Year after her recent work with dogs in Romania, performing eye surgeries and campaigning to rescue street dogs. She had some fascinating tales to tell, and Halley allowed herself to give her full attention to everyone else at the table, because it was easier than turning to talk to Archer. Because if she turned to talk to him, she was afraid that something might slip out that she didn't want to slip out. So strangers were easier.

She spoke to one guy called Rupert, who'd spent some time out in Africa tagging rhinos, Wes, who'd been abroad campaigning to stop bear bile farms, and a young veterinary nurse, like herself, who'd been working hard in her own practice to try and bring down incidents of animal diabetes by educating owners on the risks. It was an incredible night, topped by delicious food. A salmon starter. A choice of lamb shank or vegetable chana for main, finishing with a sorbet or lemon meringue pie.

Halley felt pleasantly full as they entered the fundraising part of the evening with a charity auction. Archer bid on a couple of items but didn't win any. But she laughed and had fun, as the auctioneer was quite a funny guy and had lots of jokes. By the time the dancing began again, she'd almost forgotten her upset of earlier and headed onto the dance floor with

Archer and got through three dances before it all became too much and she felt *exhausted*.

'Let's go home,' he whispered in her ear.

She readily agreed, looking forward to the idea of her own bed immensely. As they drove home, they sang along to songs on the radio and Halley realised that all she had to do to be happy was to stop thinking so much. To stop analysing everything between her and Archer. To just *do* and enjoy and be *present*.

When they reached the cottage, she kicked off her heels with a heavenly sigh and headed into the kitchen to get herself a glass of water that she could take up to bed with her.

'It was a good night, wasn't it?' Archer asked.

'It was! A lot of money got raised, so that was great.'

'And you enjoyed yourself?'

'I did. Yes. There were so many fascinating people to talk to and the house itself was beautiful.'

He nodded. 'I thought you looked beautiful, too.'

She blushed slightly and turned to face him. 'That's very nice of you to say so.'

'You look beautiful every day.'

Halley paused, uncertain of what to do or say. She so much wanted to stay and explore this conversation, but it might take them both into waters too deep for either of them to swim in. And they needed to be sensible now. The magical night was over. Reality beckoned. 'Thank you. But I think we ought to say good-night now.'

He nodded and stepped away, so she could pass him.

The tension ratcheted up as she passed him by, falling again as she made her way upstairs away from him. She could breathe again. Freely. Archer saying she looked beautiful every day was just the kind of thing she wanted to hear, but it was dangerous talk. And she didn't want to be in any kind of danger. Not with him. Not whilst it was so good.

She got to her room and closed the door behind her, leaning back against it and sighing heavily before she pushed off it and headed over to her wardrobe to undo her dress and get into her robe. Did she have any energy to read for a little while? She'd been tired before and needed to come home, but Archer's comments had fired her up again and she suddenly felt more alive than she'd felt all evening.

She got into bed and picked up her book. One of the ones that he'd bought for her at that bookstore Many Worlds. She tried her best to concentrate on the words, but she couldn't.

She could hear Archer moving about. Switching off lights downstairs. His footsteps on the stairs as he came up to his own room. His pause outside her bedroom door.

That pause suggested way too much.

That pause suggested that maybe he wanted to say something else. But what? What did he want to say?

She couldn't bear it. It was too much. Halley threw off her covers, went to her bedroom door and opened it, ready to confront him, ready to tell him that he couldn't say nice things like that to her, because it was far too risky! Far too dangerous!

But when she opened her bedroom door and saw his face…she faltered.

He looked to be in some kind of pain. Emotional pain. He looked at her with such longing, with such a need that mirrored her own, she threw all caution to the wind and stepped close to kiss him. Her hands went into his hair as he kissed her back with just as much passion as she was kissing him. She staggered backwards as he pushed her towards the bed and began undoing the buttons of his shirt as he laid her down upon her bed, pushing her book onto the floor with a thump.

'Archer…' There was so much to say. So much she needed to say.

'Do you want me to stop?' he whispered, breathing heavily.

'No.' No, she did not. Maybe later she would regret saying no, but right now? In this moment? All she wanted was him and she felt absolutely sure that he felt the same way.

We can do this. We can find a way to make this work!

He peeled off his shirt and this time, she saw how beautiful he was. The last time it had been dark. Moonlight her only visual aid as they'd made out on Rookery Point. But here? In her bedroom? With the lights on? His musculature was a thing to see. Amazing to touch. She ran her fingertips down his chest, over his sensitive stomach and down. Down towards his belt where she could see and feel that he wanted her. 'Do you want *me* to stop?' she asked, her voice breathy.

He shook his head. 'No.'

She smiled then. Smiled a victory. He was hers and she was his. Exactly how it should be.

Halley made short work of the buckle. His trouser button. His zip. Archer shucked off his trousers, his socks, then he was peeling back her robe to gaze down on her, his lips swiftly following his gaze as he trailed his mouth over her breasts. Her nipples. The underside. Kissing and licking his way over her gently rounded belly and down to the top of her underwear. The last barrier that either of them wore.

He looked up at her as he slid it down her legs. Continued staring at her as he removed his own jersey boxers.

And then he lay on top of her and she could feel every delicious inch of him.

And she was determined she would enjoy it all.

CHAPTER TEN

ARCHER WAS LYING THERE, staring at the ceiling as the morning's early rays began to filter into the room, worrying. Last night had been…amazing. Electrifying! All he'd been dreaming of, thinking of, had happened and he'd thoroughly enjoyed every minute. Halley had too. At least he hoped. But what the hell did it mean? One lapse. Giving in to his physical need for her… Had it ruined everything? Maybe she had just been scratching an itch, too? He'd read somewhere that pregnant women could experience a surge in their sex drives. Was that what last night had been?

He turned to look at her, lying beside him. They'd begun in her room. Had sex, made it to the shower room, soaped each other down in there and then carried on in his bedroom. It was as if they'd been unable to get enough of each other. As if they'd been filling up on how it felt.

*Because we both know it can't happen
again? Because we both know it* shouldn't
happen again?

His mobile phone at the side of the bed
beeped and, groaning, he reached over for it
and glanced at the screen. It was the out of
hours emergency line. Not wanting to disturb
Halley, who looked deeply asleep, he quickly
got out of bed and went to stand in the hall,
closing the bedroom door behind him.

'Hello?'

It was James. 'Sorry to wake you, Archer,
but we've had Sylvie Campbell on the phone.
She's got a pygmy goat struggling to give birth
and she needs someone to go out to the farm.
I'd go, but I need to stay here to monitor our
overnight patients. Suzie's oxygen levels keep
tanking.'

Suzie was a black lab that had come in with
terrible breathing problems yesterday. 'Oh,
okay. Call her back and let her know I'll be
there in ten minutes.'

'Okay, thanks.'

He ended the call and hurried downstairs,
grabbing unpressed clothes from the laundry
basket in the utility room. He pulled on boots
and grabbed his keys and hurried from the
house, glad to be out. Glad to be in the fresh

air, away from Halley, where he could think clearly.

What they'd done last night didn't have to change anything. Not really. They could carry on as if it never happened. Sure, the next few days might feel a little odd, but they could do it, right? She'd been tired. They'd had a big night out together, which had been really nice. They'd danced together, which might have created a false belief that something else was happening and maybe Halley just got carried away? She didn't want anything permanent and he knew that for sure, because before they'd gone to bed he'd told her how beautiful she was.

She'd said, 'Thank you. But I think we ought to say goodnight now.'

She didn't want to pursue a relationship with him. Not in that way. Otherwise she would have made it clear! She would have responded. She might have told him that she thought he looked handsome, too, or whatever. But she hadn't. She'd shut him down. Walked away. Created space. He was the one that had pushed. He was the one that had given her a compliment without thinking first. He was the one that had paused outside her bedroom door, in complete agony, because all he'd wanted was to be in her room with her, rather than in his own room, alone.

How many nights had he lain in his bed, knowing she was just in the next room? There was so much he wanted to say, so much that he wanted to change between them, but he didn't think that she wanted him in that way. Sex was fine. Sex was easy. It was a short-term thing. You could even distance yourself from it, if you wanted, but a full-on relationship? Something long term? Something much more committed? That was the big question, and not once had she said she was ready for it, even though he felt that maybe they would have a chance. For some reason, he felt, deep down in his soul, that he and Halley could work.

But she'd given him no sign that that was what she wanted and so he needed to pull himself back again. Put himself back into that box that said he was just the father to her child and her friend and nothing more, because having Halley as a friend was much better than not having Halley at all.

They'd had a minor slip, that was all.

A breach of their control. A lovely breach, but a breach, a mistake, an erroneous event that he didn't think should ruin anything. They were adult enough to move on.

When he arrived at Campbell's farm, Sylvie ·

was waiting for him in the pygmy goat shed where she bedded them down at night. The goat mother that was struggling was isolated from the others in a small pen, with Sylvie looking on, clutching a mug of steaming tea. 'She's been like this for hours. Keeps trying to push, but nothing's moving. I see hooves, but they keep retracting after each contraction and I'm just worried that it's a really big kid in there.'

'Have you tried to assist?'

'Yes, but since the op, I can't stay kneeling, or bent over long enough to pull so hard.'

'No. We don't need you hurting yourself. Give me a few minutes to get on some gloves and I'll examine her and see what we've got. Hopefully we won't need to do a C-section.'

'You left Halley at home, then?'

'Er, yeah. She was sleeping. I mean, I assume she was sleeping.' He felt heat rise to his cheeks, but Sylvie didn't notice as her phone beeped.

'Oh! Speak of the devil. She's up.' And Sylvie began tapping out a message. 'I'll tell her you're here.'

Archer nodded. Maybe that was a good thing? That way, Halley would know that he hadn't just run out on her. That he was out working. He climbed into the pen, donned his gloves and began to palpate the mother goat. It did feel as if a large kid was coming first and he really didn't want to have to perform a C-section if he could avoid it. He watched her go through a contraction and it was exactly as Sylvie said. The front hooves appeared and disappeared with each contraction. If he could get hold of them and help pull, then maybe they could safely deliver the kid if he could get the head and shoulders out?

Kneeling beside the goat, he waited for the next contraction and tried to hold onto the hooves to help pull the kid out, but there was a lot of fluid, and the hooves were slippery, and he knew he'd need rope. He'd delivered a calf once from a cow the same way, back in his veterinary medicine early days.

'Have you got any rope, Sylvie?'

'Yes, love. Hang on, I'll go get it.'

Archer soothed the goat as she struggled, stroking her fur and whispering gently to her. He knew the second twin was much smaller and that delivery should go smoother. They just needed to get this one out.

When Sylvie arrived with the rope, he tied it around the front hooves and waited for the next contraction and then began to pull. It was a fine line to walk. He didn't want to pull so hard he'd tear the goat internally, but he needed to pull hard enough to have an effect and help those wider shoulders and head pass through the canal. Ensuring a safe delivery would also help prevent future problems as he knew of goats that had suffered with a birthing dystocia before ended up with milk fever, or mastitis, a toxaemia or even a prolapsed uterus. There were many complications and he hoped to avoid them. Helping her now would give her extra energy for the second kid.

The goat kept bleating, calling out in discomfort as he pulled, but he knew he had to do it if both mother and kid were to get through this. The rope was helping and with each contraction he helped the mother with his pulling as she pushed, and there was a moment, an ever so brief moment, when he felt as if this was going to have to be surgical, before he felt the shoulders and head shift past that difficult spot in the mother's hips and the kid slid out in a whoosh of fluid and birthing sac.

'Yes! There we go! Sylvie, can you hand me that towel?' He helped clean some of the fluids off the kid as the mother turned and began washing her baby.

It let out a tiny bleat and shook its head, its two floppy ears wetly flapping around as its mother washed it, seemingly unperturbed by the assisted delivery.

'Oh, thank you, Archer!'

'She did all the work.'

'But you saved her.'

'She just needed a little extra push. Sometimes they're afraid to push past the pain.'

Sylvie nodded. 'We all can be like that. I think you deserve a treat. Want a coffee? I bet you've not had a drink yet this morning.'

He looked at her and nodded. 'Coffee sounds great.'

'I'll make you some breakfast, too. You okay to stay and watch her with the second kid?'

'Knowing breakfast is coming? You bet.'

'Come on in when it's all done. You know the way.'

'Thanks.' He watched Sylvie leave and disappear into the house just as a car pulled up. It looked like a taxi, and he briefly wondered who was visiting the farm that early when Halley stepped out.

Just seeing her made him go all hot and flustered. He'd not expected to see her yet. He'd not thought of what he could say to her.

But he saw her looking around and she must have spotted the lamp on in the shed as she came on over, wrapping her coat around her in the chill morning air.

'You were gone when I woke up.'

'Emergency delivery. I didn't want to wake you.'

No. I wanted to hold you close. Spoon you. Kiss you. But couldn't.

'I thought… I thought you'd panicked.'

He made a short scoffing noise, without looking at her. 'About what?'

'About us. About what we did.'

He looked at her then, saw the fear on her face. Decided to let her off the hook, no matter how hard it was for him to say the words. 'We didn't do anything.'

'We slept together, Archer.'

'But it means nothing! It doesn't mean that anything has to change. I know we promised no flirting, no relationship, but we just scratched an itch, that's all. Nothing more. I'm not going to get worked up about it if you're not.' He hated lying. Hated saying these words. Because he did want to get worked up about it. He wanted to celebrate it. Tell the world that what they had was real!

'But…'

He waited for her to say more, but she didn't. She seemed to be floundering.

'Last night meant nothing to you?'

He thought she was asking because she was clarifying his position. He thought she was confirming how she felt about it too. 'Halley, last night was great, but no, it meant nothing,' he lied.

The goat was beginning to strain again. The second kid was coming. And so he hunkered down to make sure this second delivery would be easier.

'I can't believe you'd say that! Why do I keep doing this to myself?' And she turned and stormed away.

He wanted to go after her, but couldn't. He had a responsibility to this goat and its baby. His own concerns would have to come second.

Archer's mind raced. Halley seemed upset that he'd said last night was nothing! But wasn't that what she'd wanted to hear? How could she want anything else of him? She'd never given any sign. Yes, they got on great and she'd danced close to him last night and the sex was amazing between them, and they could laugh together and gaze at the stars and read the same books and have a child together, but...

Did she want more than that?

He was confused, because she'd always said she didn't!

She is living in my house. Having my child.

Had things changed? Because if he could have a future with Halley, then…

No. It's wrong of me to even hope! It would be amazing, but…what if I lost her? What if I lost them? If it all went wrong and she took my baby with her…

He felt terrified, but he had to concentrate on this birthing goat. This second kid was coming much easier. The front hooves and the head were already out, the goat bleating in between trying to chomp on bits of straw. And then with a big push, the rest of the kid slithered out and suddenly there were twins. The first was already up on its feet, shaky and shivering still, whilst its mum cleaned up the latest one. It was done. It was over. But he needed to stay to make sure both kids latched onto Mum. That she had no post-partum issues.

Maybe he was reading the situation with Halley all wrong, anyway. Maybe she didn't want him to be more than they were, maybe she just wanted to hear that the sex had meant something. That he wouldn't just count it as another notch on his bedpost. Maybe he should go and find her and tell her that of course last night had been amazing and of course she meant something to him. She was the mother of his child! But he would make her see that they were both adults here. Able to separate the physical from the emotional. Even if he was lying to himself.

Is that what my future is going to be? Lies?

Because he shouldn't have to live like that. Hiding away what he felt for her. No, it might not be what she wanted to hear and, yes, she might think that they had made a mistake in moving in together, but he had to be able to tell her his truth.

And what if she did want more from him? What if she'd been lying to herself, too?

Once he was convinced the mother goat and her twins were fine, he packed up his equipment and, with heart pounding madly, returned it to his car, then went looking for Halley. No doubt she'd be in the house with Sylvie. Exasperated? Mad?

But when he went inside, he saw Sylvie drying her hands in the kitchen alone. 'Where's Halley?'

'She went upstairs to her room. I don't know what you said to her, but she's pretty upset.'

'I told her a lie. But I want to tell her the truth. Do you mind if I go up?'

'Truth is always better. Be my guest, love.'

He kicked off his boots in case they were dirty and ran up the stairs, calling Halley's name.

She was sat on her old bed, sniffing and

wiping her eyes with a tissue. It broke his heart to see her so upset.

'I lied to you.'

'Just go away, Archer.'

'No. I need you to hear me. I lied to you just now. When I said that last night didn't mean anything. Because it wasn't true. It meant *everything* to me.'

She frowned, looking confused. 'I don't...' She sniffed, dabbed at her eyes. 'Say more.'

'Being with you...you make me feel whole. You make me feel like anything is possible. You make me think that *we* could be possible.' He paused to take a breath, to gauge how she was reacting to his words.

She didn't seem to be on the verge of telling him to shut up, so he ploughed on.

'Ever since I was a little boy, you brightened my world. I didn't think I was deserving of you back then. I was nothing. A weak kid with nothing to offer you. But when you came back into my life and we made this baby... I told you we could raise it as co-parents without any of the confusing romantic details, because I was afraid of how I might feel if I lost either of you. I kept lying and saying we could be adult about it, but I'm not sure that I can, because every time I look at you I still feel like I'm that weak little kid and that I'm not good enough for you. Not strong enough. Not enough to protect you! That you would leave, that you might walk away, and so, to keep you close, I told you I could deal with it. And I was lying.'

'You're saying that you have feelings for me?'

'No. I'm saying that I love you. I have always loved you and I will always love you. You're my star. You're my reason for getting up every morning. You're my hope. You're my heart and I don't want to be without you. I want us to be together. I want you in my bed every night. I want you to be the first thing I see in the morning and the last thing I see every night. I want to hold you in my arms and keep you safe and I want us to raise our child as a mum and dad who love one another.' He paused. 'But if that is too much for you to accept, then I will step back and I will hold all those feelings inside, as long as you stay and let me see my child.'

'I don't want that,' she whispered.

'Which part?' he asked, confused.

'Living together, but apart.'

Archer shook his head. 'I'm sorry, but I'm going to need you to spell this out for me. What do you want?'

She stood up and gave him a shy smile. 'I

want you, Archer Forde! I want all of what you said and more. Because I've been hiding how I felt, too. I thought it was hormones, I thought it was the baby making me feel this way about you, but it's not! The idea that we could live in the same house for the rest of our lives lying about how we truly felt, because we were both afraid, is terrifying to me! I've always been so afraid of making a mistake in front of the whole village again, I kept hiding my feelings from you without realising I was making the biggest mistake of my life!'

She stepped closer again, until they were mere inches apart. 'I love you with all my heart and I want us to be together. As a couple. I don't think either of us needs to be alone ever again.'

He pulled her towards him then and kissed her. Kissed her with a passion and a need that he no longer had to hold back.

She was his everything and, though once he'd felt he would always be alone, that he *wanted* to be alone, he now knew that he never could and nor did he ever want that.

He had evolved. His happiness had been in front of him his entire life. All he'd needed was a little bravery to reach out and take what was his.

His heart. His love.

Their love. It had called out to him across the many years that they'd been apart, but now, like a star, she had returned to his orbit.

Exactly where she was meant to be.

He pulled back. Smiled. Looked deeply into her eyes. 'Marry me.'

EPILOGUE

IT WAS THE perfect day for a spring wedding. The church looked spectacular as Halley arrived in her bridal car. Grey stone, outlined against the blue sky. The trees were full of cherry blossom and daffodils and narcissus carpeted the grass.

The photographer flitted around her like a hummingbird, taking pictures from this angle, then that, as she alighted from the car in her long white dress, her veil trailing behind her.

She stared at the church. She'd been here before in a white dress. She'd gone into this church full of infatuation and high hopes. In that church, her life had once been cruelly changed.

Archer had suggested that, if it bothered her, they could get married in another church, or in a park, or on the village green if she so wanted, but no. A part of her needed to vanquish the ghost of Piotr. A part of her wanted to be able to stick two fingers up at her past and prove to everyone that she was worthy of a happy ever after. That they didn't have to look down on her with pity as that girl that got jilted. To say, *Look, I got my happy. I found my love.*

Jenny and Hillary were her bridesmaids and they looked stunning in their burgundy dresses, holding miniature versions of her own bouquet.

'Is he here? Is he inside?' she asked Hills.

'He is. And he looks amazing in his suit.'

She smiled. 'He looks amazing in muddy overalls.'

'Well, thankfully, he's not wearing those. Mum would have a fit.'

'Yes, I would.' Her mum got out of the bridal car and stood beside her, holding out the crook of her elbow for Halley to slip her arm through.

She had no dad to walk her down the aisle, and that made her sad. He would have loved this, had he lived. But it felt right that her mum was doing it instead.

'Is Eliana okay?' Halley asked Hills. Their daughter had been born two months ago. Perfectly happy. Perfectly healthy. Doted on by two grateful, overwhelmed parents. Archer would do anything for her and was a great hands-on dad. No doubt, as she grew, Eliana would have her father wrapped easily around her little finger and would become a daddy's girl.

'Stephen has her with the twins.' Stephen was Hillary's husband. 'So she's in experienced hands, don't worry.'

'Okay. Let's do this.' They walked up the pathway to the church, the organ music growing louder with every step. They stopped to fiddle with her veil and dress, making it look perfect for her entrance into the church. They'd invited everyone they knew. Friends. Family. Clients. Regular visitors to the farm. The church was fit to bursting at the seams.

And then 'Wedding March' began and the doors swung open and Halley stepped into the church, with her mother at her side.

All eyes turned upon her and, though that was scary, she knew she could do it. She could get through this because she knew she had a guy standing at the end of the aisle who loved her more than anything in the world. Except maybe for his daughter!

She saw him, dressed in a dark blue suit, and he turned to look at her approach and there were tears in his eyes. He wiped the happy tears away with his finger and tried to steady himself with deep breathing.

He did indeed look amazing! And she couldn't believe she was so lucky!

As she came to stand alongside him, he leaned in and whispered, 'You look beautiful.'

She smiled shyly and passed her bouquet to Jenny as the ceremony started.

'And if there is anyone here present who has reason as to why these two may not be joined in holy matrimony, then speak now, or for ever hold your peace.'

Halley knew there wouldn't be anyone. Not this time. That the church congregation would be silent. And she smiled in triumph.

Her happy ever after was never in doubt. Not with Archer by her side. He was the most honest, the most truthful, the most loyal and loving man she could ever have met.

And he was all hers.

As she slid the ring onto his finger and said her vows, her voice broke. She loved him so much and was so happy to tell the whole village, the whole world, just how much happiness and peace Archer Forde had brought her.

Neither of them needed to be alone ever again.

* * * * *

Look out for the next story in the
Yorkshire Village Vets duet

Sparks Fly with the Single Dad
by Kate Hardy

And if you enjoyed this story, check out
these other great reads from Louisa Heaton

Snowed In with the Children's Doctor
Second Chance for the Village Nurse
The Brooding Doc and the Single Mom

All available now!